I0654565

STORIES IN LIGHT AND SHADOW

BRET HARTE

1st WORLD
LIBRARY
Literary Society

Stories in Light and Shadow

Bret Harte

© 1st World Library, 2008
PO Box 2211
Fairfield, IA 52556
www.1stworldlibrary.com
First Edition

LCCN: 2007935360

Softcover ISBN: 978-1-4218-9314-3
Hardcover ISBN: 978-1-4218-9414-0
eBook ISBN: 978-1-4218-9214-6

Purchase *"Stories in Light and Shadow"*
as a traditional bound book at:
www.1stWorldLibrary.com/purchase.asp?ISBN=978-1-4218-9314-3

1st World Library is a literary, educational organization
dedicated to:

- Creating a free internet library of downloadable ebooks

- Hosting writing competitions and offering book publishing
scholarships.

Interested in more 1st World Library books? contact:
literacy@1stworldlibrary.com
Check us out at: www.1stworldlibrary.com

1ˢᵗ World Library Literary Society

Giving Back to the World

"If you want to work on the core problem, it's early school literacy."

- James Barksdale, former CEO of Netscape

"No skill is more crucial to the future of a child, or to a democratic and prosperous society, than literacy."

- Los Angeles Times

"Literacy... means far more than learning how to read and write... The aim is to transmit... knowledge and promote social participation."

- UNESCO

"Literacy is not a luxury, it is a right and a responsibility. If our world is to meet the challenges of the twenty-first century we must harness the energy and creativity of all our citizens."

- President Bill Clinton

"Parents should be encouraged to read to their children, and teachers should be equipped with all available techniques for teaching literacy, so the varying needs and capacities of individual kids can be taken into account."

- Hugh Mackay

CONTENTS

"UNSER KARL"

The American consul for Schlachtstadt had just turned out of the broad Konig's Allee into the little square that held his consulate. Its residences always seemed to him to wear that singularly uninhabited air peculiar to a street scene in a theatre. The facades, with their stiff, striped wooden awnings over the windows, were of the regularity, color, and pattern only seen on the stage, and conversation carried on in the street below always seemed to be invested with that perfect confidence and security which surrounds the actor in his painted desert of urban perspective. Yet it was a peaceful change to the other byways and highways of Schlachtstadt which were always filled with an equally unreal and mechanical soldiery, who appeared to be daily taken out of their boxes of "caserne" or "depot" and loosely scattered all over the pretty linden-haunted German town. There were soldiers standing on street corners; soldiers staring woodenly into shop windows; soldiers halted suddenly into stone, like lizards, at the approach of Offiziere; Offiziere lounging stiffly four abreast, sweeping the pavement with their trailing sabres all at one angle. There were cavalcades of red hussars, cavalcades of blue hussars, cavalcades of Uhlans, with glittering lances and pennons—with or without a band—formally parading; there were straggling "fatigues" or "details" coming round the corners; there were dusty, businesslike columns of infantry, going nowhere and to no purpose. And they one and all seemed to be WOUND UP—for that service—and apparently always in the same place. In the band of their caps—invariably of one pattern—was a button, in the centre of which was a square opening or keyhole. The consul was always convinced that through this keyhole opening, by means of a key, the humblest caporal wound up his file, the Hauptmann controlled his lieutenants and non-commissioned officers, and even the general himself, wearing the same cap, was subject through his cap to a higher moving power. In the suburbs, when the supply of soldiers gave out, there were sentry-boxes; when these dropped off, there were "caissons," or commissary wagons. And, lest the military idea should ever fail from out the Schlachtstadt's burgher's mind, there were police in uniform, street-sweepers in uniform; the ticket-takers, guards, and sweepers at the Bahnhof were in uniform,—but all wearing the same kind of cap, with the probability of having been wound up freshly each morning for their daily work. Even the postman delivered peaceful invoices to the consul with his side-arms and the air of bringing dispatches from the field of battle; and the consul saluted, and felt for a few moments the whole weight of his consular responsibility.

Yet, in spite of this military precedence, it did not seem in the least inconsistent with the decidedly peaceful character of the town, and this again suggested its utter unreality; wandering cows sometimes got mixed up with squadrons of cavalry, and did not seem to mind it; sheep passed singly between files of infantry, or preceded them in a flock when on the march; indeed, nothing could be more delightful and innocent than to see a regiment of infantry in heavy marching order, laden with every conceivable thing they could want for a week, returning after a cheerful search for an invisible enemy in the suburbs, to bivouac peacefully among the cabbages in the market-place. Nobody was ever imposed upon for a moment by their tremendous energy and severe display; drums might beat, trumpets blow, dragoons charge furiously all over the Exercier Platz, or suddenly flash their naked swords in the streets to the guttural command of an officer—nobody seemed to mind it. People glanced up to recognize Rudolf or Max "doing their service," nodded, and went about their business. And although the officers always wore their side-arms, and at the most peaceful of social dinners only relinquished their swords in the hall, apparently that they might be ready to buckle them on again and rush out to do battle for the Fatherland between the courses, the other guests only looked upon these weapons in the light of sticks and umbrellas, and possessed their souls in peace. And when, added to this singular incongruity, many of these warriors were spectacled, studious men, and, despite their lethal weapons, wore a slightly professional air, and were—to a man—deeply sentimental and singularly simple, their attitude in this eternal Kriegspiel seemed to the consul more puzzling than ever.

As he entered his consulate he was confronted with another aspect of Schlachtstadt quite as wonderful, yet already familiar to him. For, in spite of these "alarums without," which, however, never seem to penetrate beyond the town itself, Schlachtstadt and its suburbs were known all over the world for the manufactures of certain beautiful textile fabrics, and many of the rank and file of those warriors had built up the fame and prosperity of the district over their peaceful looms in wayside cottages. There were great depots and counting-houses, larger than even the cavalry barracks, where no other uniform but that of the postman was known. Hence it was that the consul's chief duty was to uphold the flag of his own country by the examination and certification of divers invoices sent to his office by the manufacturers. But, oddly enough, these business messengers were chiefly women,—not clerks, but ordinary household servants, and, on busy days, the consulate might have been mistaken for a female registry office, so filled and possessed it was by waiting Madchen. Here it was that Gretchen, Lieschen, and Clarchen, in the cleanest of blue gowns, and stoutly but smartly shod, brought their invoices in a piece of clean paper, or folded in a blue handkerchief, and laid them, with fingers more or less worn and stubby from hard service, before the consul for his signature. Once, in the case of a very young Madchen, that signature was blotted by the sweep of a flaxen braid upon it as the child turned to go; but generally there was a grave, serious business instinct and sense of responsibility in these girls of ordinary peasant origin which, equally with their sisters of France, were unknown to the English or American woman of any class.

That morning, however, there was a slight stir among those who, with their knitting, were waiting their turn in the outer office as the vice-consul ushered the police inspector into the consul's private office. He was in uniform, of course, and it took him a moment to recover from his habitual stiff, military salute,—a little stiffer than that of the actual soldier.

It was a matter of importance! A stranger had that morning been arrested in the town and identified as a military deserter. He claimed to be an American citizen; he was now in the outer office, waiting the consul's interrogation.

The consul knew, however, that the ominous accusation had only a mild significance here. The term "military deserter" included any one who had in youth emigrated to a foreign country without first fulfilling his military duty to his fatherland. His first experiences of these cases had been tedious and difficult,—involving a reference to his Minister at Berlin, a correspondence with the American State Department, a condition of unpleasant tension, and finally the prolonged detention of some innocent German— naturalized—American citizen, who had forgotten to bring his papers with him in revisiting his own native country. It so chanced, however, that the consul enjoyed the friendship and confidence of the General Adlerkreutz, who commanded the 20th Division, and it further chanced that the same Adlerkreutz was as gallant a soldier as ever cried Vorwarts! at the head of his men, as profound a military strategist and organizer as ever carried his own and his enemy's plans in his iron head and spiked helmet, and yet with as simple and unaffected a soul breathing under his gray mustache as ever issued from the lips of a child. So this grim but gentle veteran had arranged with the consul that in cases where the presumption of nationality was strong, although the evidence was not present, he would take the consul's parole for the appearance of the "deserter" or his papers, without the aid of prolonged diplomacy. In this way the consul had saved to Milwaukee a worthy but imprudent brewer, and to New York an excellent sausage butcher and possible alderman; but had returned to martial duty one or two tramps or journeymen who had never seen America except from the decks of the ships in which they were "stowaways," and on which they were returned,—and thus the temper and peace of two great nations were preserved.

"He says," said the inspector severely, "that he is an American citizen, but has lost his naturalization papers. Yet he has made the damaging admission to others that he lived several years in Rome! And," continued the inspector, looking over his shoulder at the closed door as he placed his finger beside his nose, "he says he has relations living at Palmyra, whom he frequently visited. Ach! Observe this unheard-of-and-not-to-be-trusted statement!"

The consul, however, smiled with a slight flash of intelligence. "Let me see him," he said.

They passed into the outer office; another policeman and a

corporal of infantry saluted and rose. In the centre of an admiring and sympathetic crowd of Dienstmadchen sat the culprit, the least concerned of the party; a stripling—a boy—scarcely out of his teens! Indeed, it was impossible to conceive of a more innocent, bucolic, and almost angelic looking derelict. With a skin that had the peculiar white and rosiness of fresh pork, he had blue eyes, celestially wide open and staring, and the thick flocculent yellow curls of the sun god! He might have been an overgrown and badly dressed Cupid who had innocently wandered from Paphian shores. He smiled as the consul entered, and wiped from his full red lips with the back of his hand the traces of a sausage he was eating. The consul recognized the flavor at once,—he had smelled it before in Lieschen's little hand-basket.

"You say you lived at Rome?" began the consul pleasantly. "Did you take out your first declaration of your intention of becoming an American citizen there?"

The inspector cast an approving glance at the consul, fixed a stern eye on the cherubic prisoner, and leaned back in his chair to hear the reply to this terrible question.

"I don't remember," said the culprit, knitting his brows in infantine thought. "It was either there, or at Madrid or Syracuse."

The inspector was about to rise; this was really trifling with the dignity of the municipality. But the consul laid his hand on the official's sleeve, and, opening an American atlas to a map of the State of New York, said to the prisoner, as he placed the inspector's hand on the sheet, "I see you know the names of the TOWNS on the Erie and New York Central Railroad. But"—

"I can tell you the number of people in each town and what

are the manufactures," interrupted the young fellow, with youthful vanity. "Madrid has six thousand, and there are over sixty thousand in"—

"That will do," said the consul, as a murmur of Wunderschon! went round the group of listening servant girls, while glances of admiration were shot at the beaming accused. "But you ought to remember the name of the town where your naturalization papers were afterwards sent."

"But I was a citizen from the moment I made my declaration," said the stranger smiling, and looking triumphantly at his admirers, "and I could vote!"

The inspector, since he had come to grief over American geographical nomenclature, was grimly taciturn. The consul, however, was by no means certain of his victory. His alleged fellow citizen was too encyclopaedic in his knowledge: a clever youth might have crammed for this with a textbook, but then he did not LOOK at all clever; indeed, he had rather the stupidity of the mythological subject he represented. "Leave him with me," said the consul. The inspector handed him a precis of the case. The cherub's name was Karl Schwartz, an orphan, missing from Schlachtstadt since the age of twelve. Relations not living, or in emigration. Identity established by prisoner's admission and record.

"Now, Karl," said the consul cheerfully, as the door of his private office closed upon them, "what is your little game? Have you EVER had any papers? And if you were clever enough to study the map of New York State, why weren't you clever enough to see that it wouldn't stand you in place of your papers?"

"Dot's joost it," said Karl in English; "but you see dot if I haf declairet mine intention of begomming a citizen, it's all the same, don't it?"

"By no means, for you seem to have no evidence of the DECLARATION; no papers at all."

"Zo!" said Karl. Nevertheless, he pushed his small, rosy, pickled-pig's-feet of fingers through his fleecy curls and beamed pleasantly at the consul. "Dot's vot's der matter," he said, as if taking a kindly interest in some private trouble of the consul's. "Dot's vere you vos, eh?"

The consul looked steadily at him for a moment. Such stupidity was by no means phenomenal, nor at all inconsistent with his appearance. "And," continued the consul gravely, "I must tell you that, unless you have other proofs than you have shown, it will be my duty to give you up to the authorities."

"Dot means I shall serve my time, eh?" said Karl, with an unchanged smile.

"Exactly so," returned the consul.

"Zo!" said karl. "Dese town—dose Schlachtstadt—is fine town, eh? Fine vomens. Goot men. Und beer und sausage. Blenty to eat and drink, eh? Und," looking around the room, "you and te poys haf a gay times."

"Yes," said the consul shortly, turning away. But he presently faced round again on the unfettered Karl, who was evidently indulging in a gormandizing reverie.

"What on earth brought you here, anyway?"

"Was it das?"

"What brought you here from America, or wherever you ran away from?"

"To see der, volks."

"But you are an ORPHAN, you know, and you have no folks living here."

"But all Shermany is mine volks,—de whole gountry, don't it? Pet your poots! How's dot, eh?"

The consul turned back to his desk and wrote a short note to General Adlerkreutz in his own American German. He did not think it his duty in the present case to interfere with the authorities or to offer his parole for Karl Schwartz. But he would claim that, as the offender was evidently an innocent emigrant and still young, any punishment or military degradation be omitted, and he be allowed to take his place like any other recruit in the ranks. If he might have the temerity to the undoubted, far-seeing military authority of suggestion making here, he would suggest that Karl was for the commissariat fitted! Of course, he still retained the right, on production of satisfactory proof, his discharge to claim.

The consul read this aloud to Karl. The cherubic youth smiled and said, "Zo!" Then, extending his hand, he added the word "Zshake!"

The consul shook his hand a little remorsefully, and, preceding him to the outer room, resigned him with the note into the inspector's hands. A universal sigh went up from the girls, and glances of appeal sought the consul; but he wisely concluded that it would be well, for a while, that Karl—a helpless orphan—should be under some sort of discipline! And the securer business of certifying invoices recommenced.

Late that afternoon he received a folded bit of blue paper from the waistbelt of an orderly, which contained in English characters and as a single word "Alright," followed by certain jagged pen-marks, which he recognized as Adlerkreutz's signature. But it was not until a week later that he learned anything definite. He was returning one night to his lodgings in the residential part of the city, and, in opening the door with his pass-key, perceived in the rear of the hall his handmaiden Trudschen, attended by the usual blue or yellow or red shadow. He was passing by them with the local 'n' Abend! on his lips when the soldier turned his face and saluted. The consul stopped. It was the cherub Karl in uniform!

But it had not subdued a single one of his characteristics. His hair had been cropped a little more closely under his cap, but there was its color and woolliness still intact; his plump figure was girt by belt and buttons, but he only looked the more unreal, and more like a combination of pen-wiper and pincushion, until his puffy breast and shoulders seemed to offer a positive invitation to any one who had picked up a pin. But, wonderful!—according to his brief story—he had been so proficient in the goose step that he had been put in uniform already, and allowed certain small privileges,—among them, evidently the present one. The consul smiled and passed on. But it seemed strange to him that Trudschen, who was a tall strapping girl, exceedingly popular with the military, and who had never looked lower than a corporal at least, should accept the attentions of an Einjahriger like that. Later he interrogated her.

Ach! it was only Unser Karl! And the consul knew he was Amerikanisch!

"Indeed!"

"Yes! It was such a tearful story!"

"Tell me what it is," said the consul, with a faint hope that Karl had volunteered some communication of his past.

"Ach Gott! There in America he was a man, and could 'vote,' make laws, and, God willing, become a town councilor,—or Ober Intendant,—and here he was nothing but a soldier for years. And this America was a fine country. Wunderschon? There were such big cities, and one 'Booflo'—could hold all Schlachtstadt, and had of people five hundred thousand!"

The consul sighed. Karl had evidently not yet got off the line of the New York Central and Erie roads. "But does he remember yet what he did with his papers?" said the consul persuasively.

"Ach! What does he want with PAPERS when he could make the laws? They were dumb, stupid things—these papers—to him."

"But his appetite remains good, I hope?" suggested the consul.

This closed the conversation, although Karl came on many other nights, and his toy figure quite supplanted the tall corporal of hussars in the remote shadows of the hall. One night, however, the consul returned home from a visit to a neighboring town a day earlier than he was expected. As he neared his house he was a little surprised to find the windows of his sitting-room lit up, and that there were no signs of Trudschen in the lower hall or passages. He made his way upstairs in the dark and pushed open the door of his apartment. To his astonishment, Karl was sitting comfortably in his own chair, his cap off before a student-lamp on the table, deeply engaged in apparent study. So profound was his abstraction that it was a moment before he looked up, and the consul had a good look at his usually beaming and responsive face, which, however, now struck him as wearing a singular air of thought and concentration. When their eyes at last met, he rose instantly and saluted, and his beaming smile returned. But, either from his natural phlegm or extraordinary self-control he betrayed neither embarrassment nor alarm.

The explanation he gave was direct and simple. Trudschen had gone out with the Corporal Fritz for a short walk, and had asked him to "keep house" during their absence. He had no books, no papers, nothing to read in the barracks, and no chance to improve his mind. He thought the Herr Consul would not object to his looking at his books. The consul was touched; it was really a trivial indiscretion and as much Trudschen's fault as Karl's! And if the poor fellow had any mind to improve,—his recent attitude certainly suggested thought and reflection,—the consul were a brute to reprove him. He smiled pleasantly as Karl returned a stubby bit of pencil and some greasy memoranda to his breast pocket, and glanced at the table. But to his surprise it was a large map that Karl had been studying, and, to his still greater surprise, a map of the consul's own district.

"You seem to be fond of map-studying," said the consul pleasantly. "You are not thinking of emigrating again?"

"Ach, no!" said Karl simply; "it is my cousine vot haf lif near here. I find her."

But he left on Trudschen's return, and the consul was surprised to see that, while Karl's attitude towards her had not changed, the girl exhibited less effusiveness than before. Believing it to be partly the effect of the return of the corporal, the consul taxed her with faithlessness. But

Trudschen looked grave.

"Ah! He has new friends, this Karl of ours. He cares no more for poor girls like us. When fine ladies like the old Frau von Wimpfel make much of him, what will you?"

It appeared, indeed, from Trudschen's account, that the widow of a wealthy shopkeeper had made a kind of protege of the young soldier, and given him presents. Furthermore, that the wife of his colonel had employed him to act as page or attendant at an afternoon Gesellschaft, and that since then the wives of other officers had sought him. Did not the Herr Consul think it was dreadful that this American, who could vote and make laws, should be subjected to such things?

The consul did not know what to think. It seemed to him, however, that Karl was "getting on," and that he was not in need of his assistance. It was in the expectation of hearing more about him, however, that he cheerfully accepted an invitation from Adlerkreutz to dine at the Caserne one evening with the staff. Here he found, somewhat to his embarrassment, that the dinner was partly in his own honor, and at the close of five courses, and the emptying of many bottles, his health was proposed by the gallant veteran Adlerkreutz in a neat address of many syllables containing all the parts of speech and a single verb. It was to the effect that in his soul-friend the Herr Consul and himself was the never-to-be-severed union of Germania and Columbia, and in their perfect understanding was the war-defying alliance of two great nations, and that in the consul's noble restoration of Unser Karl to the German army there was the astute diplomacy of a great mind. He was satisfied that himself and the Herr Consul still united in the great future, looking down upon a common brotherhood,—the great Germanic-American Confederation,—would feel satisfied with them-selves and each other and their never-to-be-forgotten earth-labors. Cries of "Hoch! Hoch!" resounded through the apartment with the grinding roll of heavy-bottomed beer-glasses, and the consul, tremulous with emotion and a reserve verb in his pocket, rose to reply. Fully embarked upon this perilous voyage, and steering wide and clear of any treacherous shore of intelligence or fancied harbor of understanding and rest, he kept boldly out at sea. He said that, while his loving adversary in this battle of compliment had disarmed him and left him no words to reply to his generous panegyric, he could not but join with that gallant soldier in his heartfelt aspirations for the peaceful alliance of both countries. But while he fully reciprocated all his host's broader and higher sentiments, he must point out to this gallant assembly, this glorious brotherhood, that even a greater tie of sympathy knitted him to the general,—the tie of kinship! For while it was well known to the present company that their gallant commander had married an Englishwoman, he, the consul, although always an American, would now for the first time confess to them that he HIMSELF was of Dutch descent on his mother's side! He would say no more, but confidently leave them in possession of the tremendous significance of this until-then-unknown fact! He sat down, with the forgotten verb still in his pocket, but the applause that followed this perfectly conclusive, satisfying, and logical climax convinced him of his success. His hand was grasped eagerly by successive warriors; the general turned and embraced him before the breathless assembly; there were tears in the consul's eyes.

As the festivities progressed, however, he found to his surprise that Karl had not only become the fashion as a military page, but that his naive stupidity and sublime simplicity was the wondering theme and inexhaustible delight of the whole barracks. Stories were told of his genius for blundering which rivaled Handy Andy's; old stories of fatuous ignorance were rearranged and fitted to "our Karl." It was "our Karl" who, on receiving a tip of two marks from the hands of a young lady to whom he had brought the bouquet of a gallant lieutenant, exhibited some hesitation, and finally said, "Yes, but, gnadiges Fraulein, that COST us nine marks!" It was "our Karl" who, interrupting the regrets of another lady that she was unable to accept his master's invitation, said politely, "Ah! what matter, Gnadigste? I have still a letter for Fraulein Kopp [her rival], and I was told that I must not invite you both." It was "our Karl" who astonished the hostess to whom he was sent at the last moment with apologies from an officer, unexpectedly detained at barrack duty, by suggesting that he should bring that unfortunate officer his dinner from the just served table. Nor were these charming infelicities confined to his social and domestic service. Although ready, mechanical, and invariably docile in the manual and physical duties of a soldier,—which endeared him to the German drill-master,—he was still invincibly ignorant as to its purport, or even the meaning and structure of the military instruments he handled or vacantly looked upon. It was "our Karl" who suggested to his instructors that in field-firing it was quicker and easier to load his musket to the muzzle at once, and get rid of its death-dealing contents at a single discharge, than to load and fire consecutively. It was "our Karl" who nearly killed the instructor at sentry drill by adhering to the letter of his instructions when that instructor had forgotten the password. It was the same Karl who, severely admonished for his recklessness, the next time added to his challenge the precaution, "Unless you instantly say 'Fatherland' I'll fire!" Yet his perfect good humor and childlike curiosity were unmistakable throughout, and incited his comrades and his superiors to show him everything in the hope of getting some characteristic comment from him. Everything and everybody were open to Karl and his good-humored simplicity.

That evening, as the general accompanied the consul down

to the gateway and the waiting carriage, a figure in uniform ran spontaneously before them and shouted "Heraus!" to the sentries. But the general promptly checked "the turning out" of the guard with a paternal shake of his finger to the over-zealous soldier, in whom the consul recognized Karl. "He is my Bursche now," said the general explanatorily. "My wife has taken a fancy to him. Ach! he is very popular with these women." The consul was still more surprised. The Frau Generalin Adlerkreutz he knew to be a pronounced Englishwoman,—carrying out her English ways, proprieties, and prejudices in the very heart of Schlachtstadt, uncompro-misingly, without fear and without reproach. That she should follow a merely foreign society craze, or alter her English household so as to admit the impossible Karl, struck him oddly.

A month or two elapsed without further news of Karl, when one afternoon he suddenly turned up at the consulate. He had again sought the consular quiet to write a few letters home; he had no chance in the confinement of the barracks.

"But by this time you must be in the family of a field-marshal, at least," suggested the consul pleasantly.

"Not to-day, but next week," said Karl, with sublime simplicity; "THEN I am going to serve with the governor commandant of Rheinfestung."

The consul smiled, motioned him to a seat at a table in the outer office, and left him undisturbed to his correspondence.

Returning later, he found Karl, his letters finished, gazing with childish curiosity and admiration at some thick official envelopes, bearing the stamp of the consulate, which were lying on the table. He was evidently struck with the contrast between them and the thin, flimsy affairs he was holding in his hand. He appeared still more impressed when the consul told him what they were.

"Are you writing to your friends?" continued the consul, touched by his simplicity.

"Ach ja!" said Karl eagerly.

"Would you like to put your letter in one of these envelopes?" continued the official.

The beaming face and eyes of Karl were a sufficient answer. After all, it was a small favor granted to this odd waif, who seemed to still cling to the consular protection. He handed him the envelope and left him addressing it in boyish pride.

It was Karl's last visit to the consulate. He appeared to have spoken truly, and the consul presently learned that he had indeed been transferred, through some high official manipulation, to the personal service of the governor of Rheinfestung. There was weeping among the Dienstmadchen of Schlachtstadt, and a distinct loss of originality and lightness in the gatherings of the gentler Hausfrauen. His memory still survived in the barracks through the later editions of his former delightful stupidities,—many of them, it is to be feared, were inventions,—and stories that were supposed to have come from Rheinfestung were described in the slang of the Offiziere as being "colossal." But the consul remembered Rheinfestung, and could not imagine it as a home for Karl, or in any way fostering his peculiar qualities. For it was eminently a fortress of fortresses, a magazine of magazines, a depot of depots. It was the key of the Rhine, the citadel of Westphalia, the "Clapham Junction" of German railways, but defended, fortified, encompassed, and controlled by the newest as well as the oldest devices of military strategy and science. Even in the pipingest time of peace, whole railway trains went into it like a rat in a trap, and might have never come out of it; it stretched out an inviting hand and arm across the river that might in the twinkling of an eye be changed into a closed fist of menace. You "defiled" into it, commanded at every step by enfilading walls; you "debouched" out of it, as you thought, and found yourself only before the walls; you "reentered" it at every possible angle; you did everything apparently but pass through it. You thought yourself well out of it, and were stopped by a bastion. Its circumvallations haunted you until you came to the next station. It had pressed even the current of the river into its defensive service. There were secrets of its foundations and mines that only the highest military despots knew and kept to themselves. In a word—it was impregnable.

That such a place could not be trifled with or misunderstood in its right-and-acute-angled severities seemed plain to every one. But set on by his companions, who were showing him its defensive foundations, or in his own idle curiosity, Karl managed to fall into the Rhine and was fished out with difficulty. The immersion may have chilled his military ardor or soured his good humor, for later the consul heard that he had visited the American consular agent at an adjacent town with the old story of his American citizenship. "He seemed," said the consul's colleague, "to be well posted about American railways and American towns, but he had no papers. He lounged around the office for a while and"—

"Wrote letters home?" suggested the consul, with a flash of reminiscence.

"Yes, the poor chap had no privacy at the barracks, and I reckon was overlooked or bedeviled."

This was the last the consul heard of Karl Schwartz directly; for a week or two later he again fell into the Rhine, this time so fatally and effectually that in spite of the efforts of his companions he was swept away by the rapid current, and thus ended his service to his country. His body was never recovered.

A few months before the consul was transferred from Schlachtstadt to another post his memory of the departed Karl was revived by a visit from Adlerkreutz. The general looked grave.

"You remember Unser Karl?" he said.

"Yes."

"Do you think he was an impostor?"

"As regards his American citizenship, yes! But I could not say more."

"So!" said the general. "A very singular thing has happened," he added, twirling his mustache. "The Inspector of police has notified us of the arrival of a Karl Schwartz in this town. It appears he is the REAL Karl Schwartz, identified by his sister as the only one. The other, who was drowned, was an impostor. Hein?"

"Then you have secured another recruit?" said the consul smilingly.

"No. For this one has already served his time in Elsass, where he went when he left here as a boy. But, Donnerwetter, why should that dumb fool take his name?"

"By chance, I fancy. Then he stupidly stuck to it, and had to take the responsibilities with it. Don't you see?" said the consul, pleased with his own cleverness.

"Zo-o!" said the general slowly, in his deepest voice. But the German exclamation has a variety of significance, according to the inflection, and Adlerkreutz's ejaculation seemed to contain them all.

*****

It was in Paris, where the consul had lingered on his way to his new post. He was sitting in a well-known cafe, among whose habitues were several military officers of high rank. A group of them were gathered round a table near him. He was idly watching them with an odd recollection of Schlachtstadt in his mind, and as idly glancing from them to the more attractive Boulevard without. The consul was getting a little tired of soldiers.

Suddenly there was a slight stir in the gesticulating group and a cry of greeting. The consul looked up mechanically, and then his eyes remained fixed and staring at the newcomer. For it was the dead Karl; Karl, surely! Karl!—his plump figure belted in a French officer's tunic; his flaxen hair clipped a little closer, but still its fleece showing under his kepi. Karl, his cheeks more cherubic than ever—unchanged but for a tiny yellow toy mustache curling up over the corners of his full lips. Karl, beaming at his companions in his old way, but rattling off French vivacities without the faintest trace of accent. Could he be mistaken? Was it some phenomenal resemblance, or had the soul of the German private been transmigrated to the French officer.

The consul hurriedly called the garcon. "Who is that officer who has just arrived?"

"It is the Captain Christian, of the Intelligence Bureau," said the waiter, with proud alacrity. "A famous officer, brave as a rabbit,—un fier lapin,—and one of our best clients. So drole, too, such a farceur and mimic. M'sieur would be ravished to hear his imitations."

"But he looks like a German; and his name!"

"Ah, he is from Alsace. But not a German!" said the waiter, absolutely whitening with indignation. "He was at Belfort. So was I. Mon Dieu! No, a thousand times no!"

"But has he been living here long?" said the consul.

"In Paris, a few months. But his Department, M'sieur understands, takes him EVERYWHERE! Everywhere where he can gain information."

The consul's eyes were still on the Captain Christian. Presently the officer, perhaps instinctively conscious of the scrutiny, looked towards him. Their eyes met. To the consul's surprise, the ci-devant Karl beamed upon him, and advanced with outstretched hand.

But the consul stiffened slightly, and remained so with his glass in his hand. At which Captain Christian brought his own easily to a military salute, and said politely:—

"Monsieur le Consul has been promoted from his post. Permit me to congratulate him."

"You have heard, then?" said the consul dryly.

"Otherwise I should not presume. For our Department makes it a business—in Monsieur le Consul's case it becomes a pleasure—to know everything."

"Did your Department know that the real Karl Schwartz has returned?" said the consul dryly.

Captain Christian shrugged his shoulders. "Then it appears that the sham Karl died none too soon," he said lightly. "And yet"—he bent his eyes with mischievous reproach upon the consul.

"Yet what?" demanded the consul sternly.

"Monsieur le Consul might have saved the unfortunate man by accepting him as an American citizen and not helping to force him into the German service."

The consul saw in a flash the full military significance of this logic, and could not repress a smile. At which Captain Christian dropped easily into a chair beside him, and as easily into broken German English:—

"Und," he went on, "dees town—dees Schlachtstadt is fine town, eh? Fine womens? Goot men? Und peer and sausage? Blenty to eat and trink, eh? Und you und te poys haf a gay times?"

The consul tried to recover his dignity. The waiter behind him, recognizing only the delightful mimicry of this adorable officer, was in fits of laughter. Nevertheless, the consul managed to say dryly:—

"And the barracks, the magazines, the commissariat, the details, the reserves of Schlachtstadt were very interesting?"

"Assuredly."

"And Rheinfestung—its plans—its details, even its dangerous foundations by the river—they were to a soldier singularly instructive?"

"You have reason to say so," said Captain Christian, curling his little mustache.

"And the fortress—you think?"

"Imprenable! Mais"—

The consul remembered General Adlerkreutz's "Zo-o," and wondered.

UNCLE JIM AND UNCLE BILLY

They were partners. The avuncular title was bestowed on them by Cedar Camp, possibly in recognition of a certain matured good humor, quite distinct from the spasmodic exuberant spirits of its other members, and possibly from what, to its youthful sense, seemed their advanced ages— which must have been at least forty! They had also set habits even in their improvidence, lost incalculable and unpayable sums to each other over euchre regularly every evening, and inspected their sluice-boxes punctually every Saturday for repairs—which they never made. They even got to resemble each other, after the fashion of old married couples, or, rather, as in matrimonial partnerships, were subject to the domination of the stronger character; although in their case it is to be feared that it was the feminine Uncle Billy— enthusiastic, imaginative, and loquacious—who swayed the masculine, steady-going, and practical Uncle Jim. They had lived in the camp since its foundation in 1849; there seemed to be no reason why they should not remain there until its inevitable evolution into a mining-town. The younger members might leave through restless ambition or a desire for change or novelty; they were subject to no such trifling mutation. Yet Cedar Camp was surprised one day to hear that Uncle Billy was going away.

The rain was softly falling on the bark thatch of the cabin

Bret Harte

with a muffled murmur, like a sound heard through sleep. The southwest trades were warm even at that altitude, as the open door testified, although a fire of pine bark was flickering on the adobe hearth and striking out answering fires from the freshly scoured culinary utensils on the rude sideboard, which Uncle Jim had cleaned that morning with his usual serious persistency. Their best clothes, which were interchangeable and worn alternately by each other on festal occasions, hung on the walls, which were covered with a coarse sailcloth canvas instead of lath-and-plaster, and were diversified by pictures from illustrated papers and stains from the exterior weather. Two "bunks," like ships' berths,— an upper and lower one,—occupied the gable-end of this single apartment, and on beds of coarse sacking, filled with dry moss, were carefully rolled their respective blankets and pillows. They were the only articles not used in common, and whose individuality was respected.

Uncle Jim, who had been sitting before the fire, rose as the square bulk of his partner appeared at the doorway with an armful of wood for the evening stove. By that sign he knew it was nine o'clock: for the last six years Uncle Billy had regularly brought in the wood at that hour, and Uncle Jim had as regularly closed the door after him, and set out their single table, containing a greasy pack of cards taken from its drawer, a bottle of whiskey, and two tin drinking-cups. To this was added a ragged memorandum-book and a stick of pencil. The two men drew their stools to the table.

"Hol' on a minit," said Uncle Billy.

His partner laid down the cards as Uncle Billy extracted from his pocket a pill-box, and, opening it, gravely took a pill. This was clearly an innovation on their regular proceedings, for Uncle Billy was always in perfect health.

"What's this for?" asked Uncle Jim half scornfully.

"Agin ager."

"You ain't got no ager," said Uncle Jim, with the assurance of intimate cognizance of his partner's physical condition.

"But it's a pow'ful preventive! Quinine! Saw this box at Riley's store, and laid out a quarter on it. We kin keep it here, comfortable, for evenings. It's mighty soothin' arter a man's done a hard day's work on the river-bar. Take one."

Uncle Jim gravely took a pill and swallowed it, and handed the box back to his partner.

"We'll leave it on the table, sociable like, in case any of the boys come in," said Uncle Billy, taking up the cards. "Well. How do we stand?"

Uncle Jim consulted the memorandum-book. "You were owin' me sixty-two thousand dollars on the last game, and the limit's seventy-five thousand!"

"Je whillikins!" ejaculated Uncle Billy. "Let me see."

He examined the book, feebly attempted to challenge the additions, but with no effect on the total. "We oughter hev made the limit a hundred thousand," he said seriously; "seventy-five thousand is only triflin' in a game like ours. And you've set down my claim at Angel's?" he continued.

"I allowed you ten thousand dollars for that," said Uncle Jim, with equal gravity, "and it's a fancy price too."

The claim in question being an unprospected hillside ten miles distant, which Uncle Jim had never seen, and Uncle

Billy had not visited for years, the statement was probably true; nevertheless, Uncle Billy retorted:—

"Ye kin never tell how these things will pan out. Why, only this mornin' I was taking a turn round Shot Up Hill, that ye know is just rotten with quartz and gold, and I couldn't help thinkin' how much it was like my ole claim at Angel's. I must take a day off to go on there and strike a pick in it, if only for luck."

Suddenly he paused and said, "Strange, ain't it, you should speak of it to-night? Now I call that queer!"

He laid down his cards and gazed mysteriously at his companion. Uncle Jim knew perfectly that Uncle Billy had regularly once a week for many years declared his final determination to go over to Angel's and prospect his claim, yet nevertheless he half responded to his partner's suggestion of mystery, and a look of fatuous wonder crept into his eyes. But he contented himself by saying cautiously, "You spoke of it first."

"That's the more sing'lar," said Uncle Billy confidently. "And I've been thinking about it, and kinder seeing myself thar all day. It's mighty queer!" He got up and began to rummage among some torn and coverless books in the corner.

"Where's that 'Dream Book' gone to?"

"The Carson boys borrowed it," replied Uncle Jim. "Anyhow, yours wasn't no dream—only a kind o' vision, and the book don't take no stock in visions." Nevertheless, he watched his partner with some sympathy, and added, "That reminds me that I had a dream the other night of being in 'Frisco at a small hotel, with heaps o' money, and all the time being sort o' scared and bewildered over it."

"No?" queried his partner eagerly yet reproachfully. "You never let on anything about it to ME! It's mighty queer you havin' these strange feelin's, for I've had 'em myself. And only to-night, comin' up from the spring, I saw two crows hopping in the trail, and I says, 'If I see another, it's luck, sure!' And you'll think I'm lyin', but when I went to the wood-pile just now there was the THIRD one sittin' up on a log as plain as I see you. Tell 'e what folks ken laugh—but that's just what Jim Filgee saw the night before he made the big strike!"

They were both smiling, yet with an underlying credulity and seriousness as singularly pathetic as it seemed incongruous to their years and intelligence. Small wonder, however, that in their occupation and environment—living daily in an atmosphere of hope, expectation, and chance, looking forward each morning to the blind stroke of a pick that might bring fortune—they should see signs in nature and hear mystic voices in the trackless woods that surrounded them. Still less strange that they were peculiarly susceptible to the more recognized diversions of chance, and were gamblers on the turning of a card who trusted to the revelation of a shovelful of upturned earth.

It was quite natural, therefore, that they should return from their abstract form of divination to the table and their cards. But they were scarcely seated before they heard a crackling step in the brush outside, and the free latch of their door was lifted. A younger member of the camp entered. He uttered a peevish "Halloo!" which might have passed for a greeting, or might have been a slight protest at finding the door closed, drew the stool from which Uncle Jim had just risen before the fire, shook his wet clothes like a Newfoundland dog, and sat down. Yet he was by no means churlish nor coarse-looking, and this act was rather one of easy-going, selfish, youthful familiarity than of rudeness. The cabin of Uncles

Billy and Jim was considered a public right or "common" of the camp. Conferences between individual miners were appointed there. "I'll meet you at Uncle Billy's" was a common tryst. Added to this was a tacit claim upon the partners' arbitrative powers, or the equal right to request them to step outside if the interviews were of a private nature. Yet there was never any objection on the part of the partners, and to-night there was not a shadow of resentment of this intrusion in the patient, good-humored, tolerant eyes of Uncles Jim and Billy as they gazed at their guest. Perhaps there was a slight gleam of relief in Uncle Jim's when he found that the guest was unaccompanied by any one, and that it was not a tryst. It would have been unpleasant for the two partners to have stayed out in the rain while their guests were exchanging private confidences in their cabin. While there might have been no limit to their good will, there might have been some to their capacity for exposure.

Uncle Jim drew a huge log from beside the hearth and sat on the driest end of it, while their guest occupied the stool. The young man, without turning away from his discontented, peevish brooding over the fire, vaguely reached backward for the whiskey-bottle and Uncle Billy's tin cup, to which he was assisted by the latter's hospitable hand. But on setting down the cup his eye caught sight of the pill-box.

"Wot's that?" he said, with gloomy scorn. "Rat poison?"

"Quinine pills—agin ager," said Uncle Jim. "The newest thing out. Keeps out damp like Injin-rubber! Take one to follow yer whiskey. Me and Uncle Billy wouldn't think o' settin' down, quiet like, in the evening arter work, without 'em. Take one—ye 'r' welcome! We keep 'em out here for the boys."

Accustomed as the partners were to adopt and wear each

other's opinions before folks, as they did each other's clothing, Uncle Billy was, nevertheless, astonished and delighted at Uncle Jim's enthusiasm over HIS pills. The guest took one and swallowed it.

"Mighty bitter!" he said, glancing at his hosts with the quick Californian suspicion of some practical joke. But the honest faces of the partners reassured him.

"That bitterness ye taste," said Uncle Jim quickly, "is whar the thing's gittin' in its work. Sorter sickenin' the malaria—and kinder water-proofin' the insides all to onct and at the same lick! Don't yer see? Put another in yer vest pocket; you'll be cryin' for 'em like a child afore ye get home. Thar! Well, how's things agoin' on your claim, Dick? Boomin', eh?"

The guest raised his head and turned it sufficiently to fling his answer back over his shoulder at his hosts. "I don't know what YOU'D call' boomin',"' he said gloomily; "I suppose you two men sitting here comfortably by the fire, without caring whether school keeps or not, would call two feet of backwater over one's claim 'boomin';' I reckon YOU'D consider a hundred and fifty feet of sluicing carried away, and drifting to thunder down the South Fork, something in the way of advertising to your old camp! I suppose YOU'd think it was an inducement to investors! I shouldn't wonder," he added still more gloomily, as a sudden dash of rain down the wide-throated chimney dropped in his tin cup—"and it would be just like you two chaps, sittin' there gormandizing over your quinine—if yer said this rain that's lasted three weeks was something to be proud of!"

It was the cheerful and the satisfying custom of the rest of the camp, for no reason whatever, to hold Uncle Jim and Uncle Billy responsible for its present location, its vicissitudes, the weather, or any convulsion of nature; and it

Bret Harte

was equally the partners' habit, for no reason whatever, to accept these animadversions and apologize.

"It's a rain that's soft and mellowin'," said Uncle Billy gently, "and supplin' to the sinews and muscles. Did ye ever notice, Jim"—ostentatiously to his partner—"did ye ever notice that you get inter a kind o' sweaty lather workin' in it? Sorter openin' to the pores!"

"Fetches 'em every time," said Uncle Billy. "Better nor fancy soap."

Their guest laughed bitterly. "Well, I'm going to leave it to you. I reckon to cut the whole concern to-morrow, and 'lite' out for something new. It can't be worse than this."

The two partners looked grieved, albeit they were accustomed to these outbursts. Everybody who thought of going away from Cedar Camp used it first as a threat to these patient men, after the fashion of runaway nephews, or made an exemplary scene of their going.

"Better think twice afore ye go," said Uncle Billy.

"I've seen worse weather afore ye came," said Uncle Jim slowly. "Water all over the Bar; the mud so deep ye couldn't get to Angel's for a sack o' flour, and we had to grub on pine nuts and jackass-rabbits. And yet—we stuck by the camp, and here we are!"

The mild answer apparently goaded their guest to fury. He rose from his seat, threw back his long dripping hair from his handsome but querulous face, and scattered a few drops on the partners. "Yes, that's just it. That's what gets me! Here you stick, and here you are! And here you'll stick and rust until you starve or drown! Here you are,—two men who ought to be out in the world, playing your part as grown men,—stuck here like children 'playing house' in the woods; playing work in your wretched mud-pie ditches, and content. Two men not so old that you mightn't be taking your part in the fun of the world, going to balls or theatres, or paying attention to girls, and yet old enough to have married and have your families around you, content to stay in this God-forsaken place; old bachelors, pigging together like poorhouse paupers. That's what gets me! Say you LIKE it? Say you expect by hanging on to make a strike—and what does that amount to? What are YOUR chances? How many of us have made, or are making, more than grub wages? Say you're willing to share and share alike as you do—have you got enough for two? Aren't you actually living off each other? Aren't you grinding each other down, choking each other's struggles, as you sink together deeper and deeper in the mud of this cussed camp? And while you're doing this, aren't you, by your age and position here, holding out hopes to others that you know cannot be fulfilled?"

Accustomed as they were to the half-querulous, half-humorous, but always extravagant, criticism of the others, there was something so new in this arraignment of them-selves that the partners for a moment sat silent. There was a slight flush on Uncle Billy's cheek, there was a slight paleness on Uncle Jim's. He was the first to reply. But he did so with a certain dignity which neither his partner nor their guest had ever seen on his face before.

"As it's OUR fire that's warmed ye up like this, Dick Bullen," he said, slowly rising, with his hand resting on Uncle Billy's shoulder, "and as it's OUR whiskey that's loosened your tongue, I reckon we must put up with what ye 'r' saying, just as we've managed to put up with our own way o' living, and not quo'll with ye under our own roof."

The young fellow saw the change in Uncle Jim's face and quickly extended his hand, with an apologetic backward shake of his long hair. "Hang it all, old man," he said, with a laugh of mingled contrition and amusement, "you mustn't mind what I said just now. I've been so worried thinking of things about MYSELF, and, maybe, a little about you, that I quite forgot I hadn't a call to preach to anybody—least of all to you. So we part friends, Uncle Jim, and you too, Uncle Billy, and you'll forget what I said. In fact, I don't know why I spoke at all—only I was passing your claim just now, and wondering how much longer your old sluice-boxes would hold out, and where in thunder you'd get others when they caved in! I reckon that sent me off. That's all, old chap!"

Uncle Billy's face broke into a beaming smile of relief, and it was HIS hand that first grasped his guest's; Uncle Jim quickly followed with as honest a pressure, but with eyes that did not seem to be looking at Bullen, though all trace of resentment had died out of them. He walked to the door with him, again shook hands, but remained looking out in the darkness some time after Dick Bullen's tangled hair and broad shoulders had disappeared.

Meantime, Uncle Billy had resumed his seat and was chuckling and reminiscent as he cleaned out his pipe.

"Kinder reminds me of Jo Sharp, when he was cleaned out at poker by his own partners in his own cabin, comin' up here and bedevilin' US about it! What was it you lint him?"

But Uncle Jim did not reply; and Uncle Billy, taking up the cards, began to shuffle them, smiling vaguely, yet at the same time somewhat painfully. "Arter all, Dick was mighty cut up about what he said, and I felt kinder sorry for him. And, you know, I rather cotton to a man that speaks his mind. Sorter clears him out, you know, of all the slumgullion that's in him. It's just like washin' out a pan o' prospecting: you pour in the water, and keep slushing it round and round, and out comes first the mud and dirt, and then the gravel, and then the black sand, and then—it's all out, and there's a speck o' gold glistenin' at the bottom!"

"Then you think there WAS suthin' in what he said?" said Uncle Jim, facing about slowly.

An odd tone in his voice made Uncle Billy look up. "No," he said quickly, shying with the instinct of an easy pleasure-loving nature from a possible grave situation. "No, I don't think he ever got the color! But wot are ye moonin' about for? Ain't ye goin' to play? It's mor' 'n half past nine now."

Thus adjured, Uncle Jim moved up to the table and sat down, while Uncle Billy dealt the cards, turning up the Jack or right bower—but WITHOUT that exclamation of delight which always accompanied his good fortune, nor did Uncle Jim respond with the usual corresponding simulation of deep disgust. Such a circumstance had not occurred before in the history of their partnership. They both played in silence—a silence only interrupted by a larger splash of raindrops down the chimney.

"We orter put a couple of stones on the chimney-top, edgewise, like Jack Curtis does. It keeps out the rain without interferin' with the draft," said Uncle Billy musingly.

"What's the use if"—

"If what?" said Uncle Billy quietly.

"If we don't make it broader," said Uncle Jim half wearily.

They both stared at the chimney, but Uncle Jim's eye

followed the wall around to the bunks. There were many discolorations on the canvas, and a picture of the Goddess of Liberty from an illustrated paper had broken out in a kind of damp, measly eruption. "I'll stick that funny handbill of the 'Washin' Soda' I got at the grocery store the other day right over the Liberty gal. It's a mighty perty woman washin' with short sleeves," said Uncle Billy. "That's the comfort of them picters, you kin always get somethin' new, and it adds thickness to the wall."

Uncle Jim went back to the cards in silence. After a moment he rose again, and hung his overcoat against the door.

"Wind's comin' in," he said briefly.

"Yes," said Uncle Billy cheerfully, "but it wouldn't seem nat'ral if there wasn't that crack in the door to let the sunlight in o mornin's. Makes a kind o' sundial, you know. When the streak o' light's in that corner, I says 'six o'clock!' when it's across the chimney I say 'seven!' and so 'tis!"

It certainly had grown chilly, and the wind was rising. The candle guttered and flickered; the embers on the hearth brightened occasionally, as if trying to dispel the gathering shadows, but always ineffectually. The game was frequently interrupted by the necessity of stirring the fire. After an interval of gloom, in which each partner successively drew the candle to his side to examine his cards, Uncle Jim said:—

"Say?"

"Well!" responded Uncle Billy.

"Are you sure you saw that third crow on the wood-pile?"

"Sure as I see you now—and a darned sight plainer. Why?"

"Nothin', I was just thinkin'. Look here! How do we stand now?"

Uncle Billy was still losing. "Nevertheless," he said cheerfully, "I'm owin' you a matter of sixty thousand dollars."

Uncle Jim examined the book abstractedly. "Suppose," he said slowly, but without looking at his partner, "suppose, as it's gettin' late now, we play for my half share of the claim agin the limit—seventy thousand—to square up."

"Your half share!" repeated Uncle Billy, with amused incredulity.

"My half share of the claim,—of this yer house, you know,—one half of all that Dick Bullen calls our rotten starvation property," reiterated Uncle Jim, with a half smile.

Uncle Billy laughed. It was a novel idea; it was, of course, "all in the air," like the rest of their game, yet even then he had an odd feeling that he would have liked Dick Bullen to have known it. "Wade in, old pard," he said. "I'm on it."

Uncle Jim lit another candle to reinforce the fading light, and the deal fell to Uncle Billy. He turned up Jack of clubs. He also turned a little redder as he took up his cards, looked at them, and glanced hastily at his partner. "It's no use playing," he said. "Look here!" He laid down his cards on the table. They were the ace, king and queen of clubs, and Jack of spades,—or left bower,—which, with the turned-up Jack of clubs,—or right bower,—comprised ALL the winning cards!

"By jingo! If we'd been playin' four-handed, say you an' me agin some other ducks, we'd have made 'four' in that deal, and h'isted some money—eh?" and his eyes sparkled. Uncle Jim, also, had a slight tremulous light in his own.

"Oh no! I didn't see no three crows this afternoon," added Uncle Billy gleefully, as his partner, in turn, began to shuffle the cards with laborious and conscientious exactitude. Then dealing, he turned up a heart for trumps. Uncle Billy took up his cards one by one, but when he had finished his face had become as pale as it had been red before. "What's the matter?" said Uncle Jim quickly, his own face growing white.

Uncle Billy slowly and with breathless awe laid down his cards, face up on the table. It was exactly the same sequence IN HEARTS, with the knave of diamonds added. He could again take every trick.

They stared at each other with vacant faces and a half-drawn smile of fear. They could hear the wind moaning in the trees beyond; there was a sudden rattling at the door. Uncle Billy started to his feet, but Uncle Jim caught his arm. "DON'T LEAVE THE CARDS! It's only the wind; sit down," he said in a low awe-hushed voice, "it's your deal; you were two before, and two now, that makes your four; you've only one point to make to win the game. Go on."

They both poured out a cup of whiskey, smiling vaguely, yet with a certain terror in their eyes. Their hands were cold; the cards slipped from Uncle Billy's benumbed fingers; when he had shuffled them he passed them to his partner to shuffle them also, but did not speak. When Uncle Jim had shuffled them methodically he handed them back fatefully to his partner. Uncle Billy dealt them with a trembling hand. He turned up a club. "If you are sure of these tricks you know you've won," said Uncle Jim in a voice that was scarcely audible. Uncle Billy did not reply, but tremulously laid down the ace and right and left bowers.

He had won!

A feeling of relief came over each, and they laughed hysterically and discordantly. Ridiculous and childish as their contest might have seemed to a looker-on, to each the tension had been as great as that of the greatest gambler, without the gambler's trained restraint, coolness, and composure. Uncle Billy nervously took up the cards again.

"Don't," said Uncle Jim gravely; "it's no use—the luck's gone now."

"Just one more deal," pleaded his partner.

Uncle Jim looked at the fire, Uncle Billy hastily dealt, and threw the two hands face up on the table. They were the ordinary average cards. He dealt again, with the same result. "I told you so," said Uncle Jim, without looking up.

It certainly seemed a tame performance after their wonderful hands, and after another trial Uncle Billy threw the cards aside and drew his stool before the fire. "Mighty queer, warn't it?" he said, with reminiscent awe. "Three times running. Do you know, I felt a kind o' creepy feelin' down my back all the time. Criky! what luck! None of the boys would believe it if we told 'em—least of all that Dick Bullen, who don't believe in luck, anyway. Wonder what he'd have said! and, Lord! how he'd have looked! Wall! what are you starin' so for?"

Uncle Jim had faced around, and was gazing at Uncle Billy's good-humored, simple face. "Nothin'!" he said briefly, and his eyes again sought the fire.

"Then don't look as if you was seein' suthin'—you give me the creeps," returned Uncle Billy a little petulantly. "Let's turn in, afore the fire goes out!"

The fateful cards were put back into the drawer, the table shoved against the wall. The operation of undressing was quickly got over, the clothes they wore being put on top of their blankets. Uncle Billy yawned, "I wonder what kind of a dream I'll have tonight—it oughter be suthin' to explain that luck." This was his "good-night" to his partner. In a few moments he was sound asleep.

Not so Uncle Jim. He heard the wind gradually go down, and in the oppressive silence that followed could detect the deep breathing of his companion and the far-off yelp of a coyote. His eyesight becoming accustomed to the semi-darkness, broken only by the scintillation of the dying embers of their fire, he could take in every detail of their sordid cabin and the rude environment in which they had lived so long. The dismal patches on the bark roof, the wretched makeshifts of each day, the dreary prolongation of discomfort, were all plain to him now, without the sanguine hope that had made them bearable. And when he shut his eyes upon them, it was only to travel in fancy down the steep mountain side that he had trodden so often to the dreary claim on the overflowed river, to the heaps of "tailings" that encumbered it, like empty shells of the hollow, profitless days spent there, which they were always waiting for the stroke of good fortune to clear away. He saw again the rotten "sluicing," through whose hopeless rifts and holes even their scant daily earnings had become scantier. At last he arose, and with infinite gentleness let himself down from his berth without disturbing his sleeping partner, and wrapping himself in his blanket, went to the door, which he noiselessly opened. From the position of a few stars that were glittering in the northern sky he knew that it was yet scarcely midnight; there were still long, restless hours before the day! In the feverish state into which he had gradually worked himself it seemed to him impossible to wait the coming of the dawn.

But he was mistaken. For even as he stood there all nature seemed to invade his humble cabin with its free and fragrant breath, and invest him with its great companionship. He felt again, in that breath, that strange sense of freedom, that mystic touch of partnership with the birds and beasts, the shrubs and trees, in this greater home before him. It was this vague communion that had kept him there, that still held these world-sick, weary workers in their rude cabins on the slopes around him; and he felt upon his brow that balm that had nightly lulled him and them to sleep and forgetfulness. He closed the door, turned away, crept as noiselessly as before into his bunk again, and presently fell into a profound slumber.

But when Uncle Billy awoke the next morning he saw it was late; for the sun, piercing the crack of the closed door, was sending a pencil of light across the cold hearth, like a match to rekindle its dead embers. His first thought was of his strange luck the night before, and of disappointment that he had not had the dream of divination that he had looked for. He sprang to the floor, but as he stood upright his glance fell on Uncle Jim's bunk. It was empty. Not only that, but his BLANKETS—Uncle Jim's own particular blankets—WERE GONE!

A sudden revelation of his partner's manner the night before struck him now with the cruelty of a blow; a sudden intelligence, perhaps the very divination he had sought, flashed upon him like lightning! He glanced wildly around the cabin. The table was drawn out from the wall a little ostentatiously, as if to catch his eye. On it was lying the stained chamois-skin purse in which they had kept the few grains of gold remaining from their last week's "clean up." The grains had been carefully divided, and half had been taken! But near it lay the little memorandum-book, open, with the stick of pencil lying across it. A deep line was drawn across the page on which was recorded their imaginary extravagant gains and losses, even to the entry of Uncle Jim's half share of the claim which he had risked and lost! Underneath were hurriedly scrawled the words:—

"Settled by YOUR luck, last night, old pard.—JAMES FOSTER."

It was nearly a month before Cedar Camp was convinced that Uncle Billy and Uncle Jim had dissolved partnership. Pride had prevented Uncle Billy from revealing his suspicions of the truth, or of relating the events that preceded Uncle Jim's clandestine flight, and Dick Bullen had gone to Sacramento by stage-coach the same morning. He briefly gave out that his partner had been called to San Francisco on important business of their own, that indeed might necessitate his own removal there later. In this he was singularly assisted by a letter from the absent Jim, dated at San Francisco, begging him not to be anxious about his success, as he had hopes of presently entering into a profitable business, but with no further allusions to his precipitate departure, nor any suggestion of a reason for it. For two or three days Uncle Billy was staggered and bewildered; in his profound simplicity he wondered if his extraordinary good fortune that night had made him deaf to some explanation of his partner's, or, more terrible, if he had shown some "low" and incredible intimation of taking his partner's extravagant bet as REAL and binding. In this distress he wrote to Uncle Jim an appealing and apologetic letter, albeit somewhat incoherent and inaccurate, and bristling with misspelling, camp slang, and old partnership jibes. But to this elaborate epistle he received only Uncle Jim's repeated assurances of his own bright prospects, and his hopes that his old partner would be more fortunate, single-handed, on the old claim. For a whole week or two Uncle Billy sulked, but his invincible optimism and good humor got the better of him, and he thought only of his old partner's good fortune. He wrote him regularly, but always to one address—a box at the San Francisco post-office, which to the simple-minded Uncle Billy suggested a certain official importance. To these letters Uncle Jim responded regularly but briefly.

From a certain intuitive pride in his partner and his affection, Uncle Billy did not show these letters openly to the camp, although he spoke freely of his former partner's promising future, and even read them short extracts. It is needless to say that the camp did not accept Uncle Billy's story with unsuspecting confidence. On the contrary, a hundred surmises, humorous or serious, but always extravagant, were afloat in Cedar Camp. The partners had quarreled over their clothes—Uncle Jim, who was taller than Uncle Billy, had refused to wear his partner's trousers. They had quarreled over cards—Uncle Jim had discovered that Uncle Billy was in possession of a "cold deck," or marked pack. They had quarreled over Uncle Billy's carelessness in grinding up half a box of "bilious pills" in the morning's coffee. A gloomily imaginative mule-driver had darkly suggested that, as no one had really seen Uncle Jim leave the camp, he was still there, and his bones would yet be found in one of the ditches; while a still more credulous miner averred that what he had thought was the cry of a screech-owl the night previous to Uncle Jim's disappearance, might have been the agonized utterance of that murdered man. It was highly characteristic of that camp—and, indeed, of others in California—that nobody, not even the ingenious theorists themselves, believed their story, and that no one took the slightest pains to verify or disprove it. Happily, Uncle Billy never knew it, and moved all unconsciously in this atmosphere of burlesque suspicion. And then a singular change took place in the attitude of the camp towards him and the disrupted partnership. Hitherto, for no reason whatever, all had agreed to put the blame upon Billy—possibly because he was present to receive it. As days passed that slight reticence and dejection in his manner, which they had at first attributed to remorse and a guilty conscience, now began to tell as absurdly in his favor. Here was poor Uncle Billy toiling though the ditches, while his selfish partner was lolling in the lap of luxury in San Francisco! Uncle Billy's glowing accounts of Uncle Jim's success only contributed to the sympathy now fully given in his behalf and their execration of the absconding partner. It was proposed at Biggs's store that a letter expressing the indignation of the camp over his heartless conduct to his late partner, William Fall, should be forwarded to him. Condolences were offered to Uncle Billy, and uncouth attempts were made to cheer his loneliness. A procession of half a dozen men twice a week to his cabin, carrying their own whiskey and winding up with a "stag dance" before the premises, was sufficient to lighten his eclipsed gayety and remind him of a happier past. "Surprise" working parties visited his claim with spasmodic essays towards helping him, and great good humor and hilarity prevailed. It was not an unusual thing for an honest miner to arise from an idle gathering in some cabin and excuse himself with the remark that he "reckoned he'd put in an hour's work in Uncle Billy's tailings!" And yet, as before, it was very improbable if any of these reckless benefactors REALLY believed in their own earnestness or in the gravity of the situation. Indeed, a kind of hopeful cynicism ran through their performances. "Like as not, Uncle Billy is still in 'cahoots' [i. e., shares] with his old pard, and is just laughin' at us as he's sendin' him accounts of our tomfoolin'."

And so the winter passed and the rains, and the days of cloudless skies and chill starlit nights began. There were still freshets from the snow reservoirs piled high in the Sierran passes, and the Bar was flooded, but that passed too, and only the sunshine remained. Monotonous as the seasons were, there was a faint movement in the camp with the stirring of the sap in the pines and cedars. And then, one day, there was a strange excitement on the Bar. Men were seen running hither and thither, but mainly gathering in a crowd on Uncle Billy's claim, that still retained the old partners' names in "The Fall and Foster." To add to the excitement, there was the quickly repeated report of a revolver, to all appearance aimlessly exploded in the air by some one on the outskirts of the assemblage. As the crowd opened, Uncle Billy appeared, pale, hysterical, breathless, and staggering a little under the back-slapping and hand-shaking of the whole camp. For Uncle Billy had "struck it rich"—had just discovered a "pocket," roughly estimated to be worth fifteen thousand dollars!

Although in that supreme moment he missed the face of his old partner, he could not help seeing the unaffected delight and happiness shining in the eyes of all who surrounded him. It was characteristic of that sanguine but uncertain life that success and good fortune brought no jealousy nor envy to the unfortunate, but was rather a promise and prophecy of the fulfillment of their own hopes. The gold was there—Nature but yielded up her secret. There was no prescribed limit to her bounty. So strong was this conviction that a long-suffering but still hopeful miner, in the enthusiasm of the moment, stooped down and patted a large boulder with the apostrophic "Good old gal!"

Then followed a night of jubilee, a next morning of hurried consultation with a mining expert and speculator lured to the camp by the good tidings; and then the very next night—to the utter astonishment of Cedar Camp—Uncle Billy, with a draft for twenty thousand dollars in his pocket, started for San Francisco, and took leave of his claim and the camp forever!

****

When Uncle Billy landed at the wharves of San Francisco he was a little bewildered. The Golden Gate beyond was obliterated by the incoming sea-fog, which had also roofed in the whole city, and lights already glittered along the gray streets that climbed the grayer sand-hills. As a Western man, brought up by inland rivers, he was fascinated and thrilled by the tall-masted seagoing ships, and he felt a strange sense of the remoter mysterious ocean, which he had never seen. But he was impressed and startled by smartly dressed men and women, the passing of carriages, and a sudden conviction that he was strange and foreign to what he saw. It had been his cherished intention to call upon his old partner in his working clothes, and then clap down on the table before him a draft for ten thousand dollars as HIS share of their old claim. But in the face of these brilliant strangers a sudden and unexpected timidity came upon him. He had heard of a cheap popular hotel, much frequented by the returning gold-miner, who entered its hospitable doors—which held an easy access to shops—and emerged in a few hours a gorgeous butterfly of fashion, leaving his old chrysalis behind him. Thence he inquired his way; hence he afterwards issued in garments glaringly new and ill fitting. But he had not sacrificed his beard, and there was still something fine and original in his handsome weak face that overcame the cheap convention of his clothes. Making his way to the post-office, he was again discomfited by the great size of the building, and bewildered by the array of little square letter-boxes behind glass which occupied one whole wall, and an equal number of opaque and locked wooden ones legibly numbered. His heart leaped; he remembered the number, and before him was a window with a clerk behind it. Uncle Billy leaned forward.

"Kin you tell me if the man that box 690 b'longs to is in?"

The clerk stared, made him repeat the question, and then turned away. But he returned almost instantly, with two or three grinning heads besides his own, apparently set behind his shoulders. Uncle Billy was again asked to repeat his question. He did so.

"Why don't you go and see if 690 is in his box?" said the first clerk, turning with affected asperity to one of the others.

The clerk went away, returned, and said with singular gravity, "He was there a moment ago, but he's gone out to stretch his legs. It's rather crampin' at first; and he can't stand it more than ten hours at a time, you know."

But simplicity has its limits. Uncle Billy had already guessed his real error in believing his partner was officially connected with the building; his cheek had flushed and then paled again. The pupils of his blue eyes had contracted into suggestive black points. "Ef you'll let me in at that winder, young fellers," he said, with equal gravity, "I'll show yer how I kin make YOU small enough to go in a box without crampin'! But I only wanted to know where Jim Foster LIVED."

At which the first clerk became perfunctory again, but civil. "A letter left in his box would get you that information," he said, "and here's paper and pencil to write it now."

Uncle Billy took the paper and began to write, "Just got here. Come and see me at"—He paused. A brilliant idea had struck him; He could impress both his old partner and the upstarts at the window; he would put in the name of the latest "swell" hotel in San Francisco, said to be a fairy dream of opulence. He added "The Oriental," and without folding the paper shoved it in the window.

"Don't you want an envelope?" asked the clerk.

"Put a stamp on the corner of it," responded Uncle Billy, laying down a coin, "and she'll go through." The clerk smiled, but affixed the stamp, and Uncle Billy turned away.

But it was a short-lived triumph. The disappointment at finding Uncle Jim's address conveyed no idea of his habitation seemed to remove him farther away, and lose his identity in the great city. Besides, he must now make good his own address, and seek rooms at the Oriental. He went thither. The furniture and decorations, even in these early days of hotel-building in San Francisco, were extravagant and over-strained, and Uncle Billy felt lost and lonely in his strange surroundings. But he took a handsome suite of rooms, paid for them in advance on the spot, and then, half frightened, walked out of them to ramble vaguely through the city in the feverish hope of meeting his old partner. At night his inquietude increased; he could not face the long row of tables in the pillared dining-room, filled with smartly dressed men and women; he evaded his bedroom, with its brocaded satin chairs and its gilt bedstead, and fled to his modest lodgings at the Good Cheer House, and appeased his hunger at its cheap restaurant, in the company of retired miners and freshly arrived Eastern emigrants. Two or three days passed thus in this quaint double existence. Three or four times a day he would enter the gorgeous Oriental with affected ease and carelessness, demand his key from the hotel-clerk, ask for the letter that did not come, go to his room, gaze vaguely from his window on the passing crowd below for the partner he could not find, and then return to the Good Cheer House for rest and sustenance. On the fourth day he received a short note from Uncle Jim; it was couched in his usual sanguine but brief and businesslike style. He was very sorry, but important and profitable business took him out of town, but he trusted to return soon and welcome his old partner. He was also, for the first time, jocose, and hoped that Uncle Billy would not "see all the sights" before he, Uncle Jim, returned. Disappointing as this procrastination was to Uncle Billy, a gleam of hope irradiated it: the letter had bridged over that gulf which seemed to yawn between them at the post-office. His old partner had accepted his visit to San Francisco without question, and had alluded to a renewal of their old intimacy. For Uncle Billy, with all his trustful simplicity, had been tortured by two harrowing doubts: one, whether Uncle Jim in his new-fledged smartness as a "city" man—such as he saw in the streets—would care for his rough companionship; the other, whether he, Uncle Billy, ought not to tell him at once of his changed fortune. But, like all weak, unreasoning men, he clung desperately to a detail—he could not forego his old idea of astounding Uncle Jim by giving him his share of the "strike" as his first intimation of it, and he doubted, with more reason perhaps, if Jim would see him after he had heard of his good fortune. For Uncle Billy had still a frightened recollection of Uncle Jim's sudden stroke for independence, and that rigid punctiliousness which had made him doggedly accept the responsibility of his extravagant stake at euchre.

With a view of educating himself for Uncle Jim's company, he "saw the sights" of San Francisco—as an overgrown and somewhat stupid child might have seen them—with great curiosity, but little contamination or corruption. But I think he was chiefly pleased with watching the arrival of the Sacramento and Stockton steamers at the wharves, in the hope of discovering his old partner among the passengers on the gang-plank. Here, with his old superstitious tendency and gambler's instinct, he would augur great success in his search that day if any one of the passengers bore the least resemblance to Uncle Jim, if a man or woman stepped off first, or if he met a single person's questioning eye. Indeed, this got to be the real occupation of the day, which he would on no account have omitted, and to a certain extent revived each day in his mind the morning's work of their old partnership. He would say to himself, "It's time to go and look up Jim," and put off what he was pleased to think were his pleasures until this act of duty was accomplished.

In this singleness of purpose he made very few and no entangling acquaintances, nor did he impart to any one the secret of his fortune, loyally reserving it for his partner's first knowledge. To a man of his natural frankness and simplicity this was a great trial, and was, perhaps, a crucial test of his devotion. When he gave up his rooms at the Oriental—as not necessary after his partner's absence—he sent a letter, with his humble address, to the mysterious lock-box of his partner without fear or false shame. He would explain it all when they met. But he sometimes treated unlucky and returning miners to a dinner and a visit to the gallery of some theatre. Yet while he had an active sympathy with and understanding of the humblest, Uncle Billy, who for many years had done his own and his partner's washing, scrubbing, mending, and cooking, and saw no degradation in it, was somewhat inconsistently irritated by menial functions in men, and although he gave extravagantly to waiters, and threw a dollar to the crossing-sweeper, there was always a certain shy avoidance of them in his manner. Coming from the theatre one night Uncle Billy was, however, seriously concerned by one of these crossing-sweepers turning hastily before them and being knocked down by a passing carriage. The man rose and limped hurriedly away; but Uncle Billy was amazed and still more irritated to hear from his companion that this kind of menial occupation was often profitable, and that at some of the principal crossings the sweepers were already rich men.

But a few days later brought a more notable event to Uncle Billy. One afternoon in Montgomery Street he recognized in one of its smartly dressed frequenters a man who had a few years before been a member of Cedar Camp. Uncle Billy's childish delight at this meeting, which seemed to bridge over his old partner's absence, was, however, only half responded to by the ex-miner, and then somewhat satirically. In the fullness of his emotion, Uncle Billy confided to him that he was seeking his old partner, Jim Foster, and, reticent of his own good fortune, spoke glowingly of his partner's brilliant expectations, but deplored his inability to find him. And just now he was away on important business. "I reckon he's got back," said the man dryly. "I didn't know he had a lock-box at the post-office, but I can give you his other address. He lives at the Presidio, at Washerwoman's Bay." He stopped and looked with a satirical smile at Uncle Billy. But the latter, familiar with Californian mining-camp nomenclature, saw nothing strange in it, and merely repeated his companion's words.

"You'll find him there! Good-by! So long! Sorry I'm in a hurry," said the ex-miner, and hurried away.

Uncle Billy was too delighted with the prospect of a speedy meeting with Uncle Jim to resent his former associate's supercilious haste, or even to wonder why Uncle Jim had not informed him that he had returned. It was not the first time that he had felt how wide was the gulf between himself and these others, and the thought drew him closer to his old partner, as well as his old idea, as it was now possible to surprise him with the draft. But as he was going to surprise him in his own boarding-house—probably a handsome one—Uncle Billy reflected that he would do so in a certain style.

He accordingly went to a livery stable and ordered a landau and pair, with a negro coachman. Seated in it, in his best and most ill-fitting clothes, he asked the coachman to take him to the Presidio, and leaned back in the cushions as they drove through the streets with such an expression of beaming gratification on his good-humored face that the passers-by smiled at the equipage and its extravagant occupant. To them it seemed the not unusual sight of the successful miner "on a spree." To the unsophisticated Uncle Billy their smiling seemed only a natural and kindly recognition of his happiness, and he nodded and smiled back to them with unsuspecting candor and innocent playfulness. "These yer 'Frisco fellers ain't ALL slouches, you bet," he added to himself half aloud, at the back of the grinning coachman.

Their way led through well-built streets to the outskirts, or rather to that portion of the city which seemed to have been overwhelmed by shifting sand-dunes, from which half-submerged fences and even low houses barely marked the line of highway. The resistless trade-winds which had marked this change blew keenly in his face and slightly chilled his ardor. At a turn in the road the sea came in sight, and sloping towards it the great Cemetery of Lone Mountain, with white shafts and marbles that glittered in the sunlight like the sails of ships waiting to be launched down that slope into the Eternal Ocean. Uncle Billy shuddered. What if it had been his fate to seek Uncle Jim there!

"Dar's yar Presidio!" said the negro coachman a few moments later, pointing with his whip, "and dar's yar Wash'woman's Bay!"

Uncle Billy stared. A huge quadrangular fort of stone with a flag flying above its battlements stood at a little distance, pressed against the rocks, as if beating back the encroaching surges; between him and the fort but farther inland was a lagoon with a number of dilapidated, rudely patched cabins or cottages, like stranded driftwood around its shore. But there was no mansion, no block of houses, no street, not another habitation or dwelling to be seen!

Uncle Billy's first shock of astonishment was succeeded by a feeling of relief. He had secretly dreaded a meeting with his old partner in the "haunts of fashion;" whatever was the cause that made Uncle Jim seek this obscure retirement affected him but slightly; he even was thrilled with a vague memory of the old shiftless camp they had both abandoned. A certain instinct—he knew not why, or less still that it might be one of delicacy—made him alight before they reached the first house. Bidding the carriage wait, Uncle Billy entered, and was informed by a blowzy Irish laundress at a tub that Jim Foster, or "Arkansaw Jim," lived at the fourth shanty "beyant." He was at home, for "he'd shprained his fut." Uncle Billy hurried on, stopped before the door of a shanty scarcely less rude than their old cabin, and half timidly pushed it open. A growling voice from within, a figure that rose hurriedly, leaning on a stick, with an attempt to fly, but in the same moment sank back in a chair with an hysterical laugh—and Uncle Billy stood in the presence of his old partner! But as Uncle Billy darted forward, Uncle Jim rose again, and this time with outstretched hands. Uncle Billy caught them, and in one supreme pressure seemed to pour out and transfuse his whole simple soul into his partner's. There they swayed each other backwards and forwards and sideways by their still clasped hands, until Uncle Billy, with a glance at Uncle Jim's bandaged ankle, shoved him by sheer force down into his chair.

Uncle Jim was first to speak. "Caught, b' gosh! I mighter known you'd be as big a fool as me! Look you, Billy Fall, do you know what you've done? You've druv me out er the streets whar I was makin' an honest livin', by day, on three crossin's! Yes," he laughed forgivingly, "you druv me out er it, by day, jest because I reckoned that some time I might run into your darned fool face,"—another laugh and a grasp of the hand,—"and then, b'gosh! not content with ruinin' my business BY DAY, when I took to it at night, YOU took to goin' out at nights too, and so put a stopper on me there! Shall I tell you what else you did? Well, by the holy poker! I owe this sprained foot to your darned foolishness and my own, for it was getting away from YOU one night after the theatre that I got run into and run over!

"Ye see," he went on, unconscious of Uncle Billy's paling face, and with a naivete, though perhaps not a delicacy, equal to Uncle Billy's own, "I had to play roots on you with that lock-box business and these letters, because I did not want you to know what I was up to, for you mightn't like it, and might think it was lowerin' to the old firm, don't yer see? I wouldn't hev gone into it, but I was played out, and I don't mind tellin' you NOW, old man, that when I wrote you that first chipper letter from the lock-box I hedn't eat anythin' for two days. But it's all right NOW," with a laugh. "Then I got into this business—thinkin' it nothin'—jest the very last thing—and do you know, old pard, I couldn't tell anybody but YOU—and, in fact, I kept it jest to tell you—I've made nine hundred and fifty-six dollars! Yes, sir, NINE HUNDRED AND FIFTY-SIX DOLLARS! solid money, in Adams and Co.'s Bank, just out er my trade."

"Wot trade?" asked Uncle Billy.

Uncle Jim pointed to the corner, where stood a large, heavy crossing-sweeper's broom. "That trade."

"Certingly," said Uncle Billy, with a quick laugh.

"It's an outdoor trade," said Uncle Jim gravely, but with no suggestion of awkwardness or apology in his manner; "and thar ain't much difference between sweepin' a crossin' with a broom and raking over tailing with a rake, ONLY—WOT

YE GET with a broom YOU HAVE HANDED TO YE, and ye don't have to PICK IT UP AND FISH IT OUT ER the wet rocks and sluice-gushin'; and it's a heap less tiring to the back."

"Certingly, you bet!" said Uncle Billy enthusiastically, yet with a certain nervous abstraction.

"I'm glad ye say so; for yer see I didn't know at first how you'd tumble to my doing it, until I'd made my pile. And ef I hadn't made it, I wouldn't hev set eyes on ye agin, old pard—never!"

"Do you mind my runnin' out a minit," said Uncle Billy, rising. "You see, I've got a friend waitin' for me outside—and I reckon"—he stammered—"I'll jest run out and send him off, so I kin talk comf'ble to ye."

"Ye ain't got anybody you're owin' money to," said Uncle Jim earnestly, "anybody follerin' you to get paid, eh? For I kin jest set down right here and write ye off a check on the bank!"

"No," said Uncle Billy. He slipped out of the door, and ran like a deer to the waiting carriage. Thrusting a twenty-dollar gold-piece into the coachman's hand, he said hoarsely, "I ain't wantin' that kerridge just now; ye ken drive around and hev a private jamboree all by yourself the rest of the afternoon, and then come and wait for me at the top o' the hill yonder."

Thus quit of his gorgeous equipage, he hurried back to Uncle Jim, grasping his ten-thousand dollar draft in his pocket. He was nervous, he was frightened, but he must get rid of the draft and his story, and have it over. But before he could speak he was unexpectedly stopped by Uncle Jim.

"Now, look yer, Billy boy!" said Uncle Jim; "I got suthin' to say to ye—and I might as well clear it off my mind at once, and then we can start fair agin. Now," he went on, with a half laugh, "wasn't it enough for ME to go on pretendin' I was rich and doing a big business, and gettin' up that lock-box dodge so as ye couldn't find out whar I hung out and what I was doin'—wasn't it enough for ME to go on with all this play-actin', but YOU, you long-legged or nary cuss! must get up and go to lyin' and play-actin', too!"

"ME play-actin'? ME lyin'?" gasped Uncle Billy.

Uncle Jim leaned back in his chair and laughed. "Do you think you could fool ME? Do you think I didn't see through your little game o' going to that swell Oriental, jest as if ye'd made a big strike—and all the while ye wasn't sleepin' or eatin' there, but jest wrastlin' yer hash and having a roll down at the Good Cheer! Do you think I didn't spy on ye and find that out? Oh, you long-eared jackass-rabbit!"

He laughed until the tears came into his eyes, and Uncle Billy laughed too, albeit until the laugh on his face became quite fixed, and he was fain to bury his head in his handkerchief.

"And yet," said Uncle Jim, with a deep breath, "gosh! I was frighted—jest for a minit! I thought, mebbe, you HAD made a big strike—when I got your first letter—and I made up my mind what I'd do! And then I remembered you was jest that kind of an open sluice that couldn't keep anythin' to yourself, and you'd have been sure to have yelled it out to ME the first thing. So I waited. And I found you out, you old sinner!" He reached forward and dug Uncle Billy in the ribs.

"What WOULD you hev done?" said Uncle Billy, after an hysterical collapse.

Uncle Jim's face grew grave again. "I'd hev—I'd—hev cl'ared out! Out er 'Frisco! out er Californy! out er Ameriky! I couldn't have stud it! Don't think I would hev begrudged ye yer luck! No man would have been gladder than me." He leaned forward again, and laid his hand caressingly upon his partner's arm—"Don't think I'd hev wanted to take a penny of it—but I—thar! I COULDN'T hev stood up under it! To hev had YOU, you that I left behind, comin' down here rollin' in wealth and new partners and friends, and arrive upon me—and this shanty—and"—he threw towards the corner of the room a terrible gesture, none the less terrible that it was illogical and inconsequent to all that had gone before—"and—and—THAT BROOM!"

There was a dead silence in the room. With it Uncle Billy seemed to feel himself again transported to the homely cabin at Cedar Camp and that fateful night, with his partner's strange, determined face before him as then. He even fancied that he heard the roaring of the pines without, and did not know that it was the distant sea.

But after a minute Uncle Jim resumed:—

"Of course you've made a little raise somehow, or you wouldn't be here?"

"Yes," said Uncle Billy eagerly. "Yes! I've got"—He stopped and stammered. "I've got—a—few hundreds."

"Oh, oh!" said Uncle Jim cheerfully. He paused, and then added earnestly, "I say! You ain't got left, over and above your d—d foolishness at the Oriental, as much as five hundred dollars?"

"I've got," said Uncle Billy, blushing a little over his first deliberate and affected lie, "I've got at least five hundred and seventy-two dollars. Yes," he added tentatively, gazing anxiously at his partner, "I've got at least that."

"Je whillikins!" said Uncle Jim, with a laugh. Then eagerly, "Look here, pard! Then we're on velvet! I've got NINE hundred; put your FIVE with that, and I know a little ranch that we can get for twelve hundred. That's what I've been savin' up for—that's my little game! No more minin' for ME. It's got a shanty twice as big as our old cabin, nigh on a hundred acres, and two mustangs. We can run it with two Chinamen and jest make it howl! Wot yer say—eh?" He extended his hand.

"I'm in," said Uncle Billy, radiantly grasping Uncle Jim's. But his smile faded, and his clear simple brow wrinkled in two lines.

Happily Uncle Jim did not notice it. "Now, then, old pard," he said brightly, "we'll have a gay old time to-night—one of our jamborees! I've got some whiskey here and a deck o' cards, and we'll have a little game, you understand, but not for 'keeps' now! No, siree; we'll play for beans."

A sudden light illuminated Uncle Billy's face again, but he said, with a grim desperation, "Not to-night! I've got to go into town. That fren' o' mine expects me to go to the theayter, don't ye see? But I'll be out to-morrow at sun-up, and we'll fix up this thing o' the ranch."

"Seems to me you're kinder stuck on this fren'," grunted Uncle Jim.

Uncle Billy's heart bounded at his partner's jealousy. "No—but I MUST, you know," he returned, with a faint laugh.

"I say—it ain't a HER, is it?" said Uncle Jim.

Uncle Billy achieved a diabolical wink and a creditable blush at his lie.

"Billy?"

"Jim!"

And under cover of this festive gallantry Uncle Billy escaped. He ran through the gathering darkness, and toiled up the shifting sands to the top of the hill, where he found the carriage waiting.

"Wot," said Uncle Billy in a low confidential tone to the coachman, "wot do you 'Frisco fellers allow to be the best, biggest, and riskiest gamblin'-saloon here? Suthin' high-toned, you know?"

The negro grinned. It was the usual case of the extravagant spendthrift miner, though perhaps he had expected a different question and order.

"Dey is de 'Polka,' de 'El Dorado,' and de 'Arcade' saloon, boss," he said, flicking his whip meditatively. "Most gents from de mines prefer de 'Polka,' for dey is dancing wid de gals frown in. But de real prima facie place for gents who go for buckin' agin de tiger and straight-out gamblin' is de 'Arcade.'"

"Drive there like thunder!" said Uncle Billy, leaping into the carriage.

*****

True to his word, Uncle Billy was at his partner's shanty early the next morning. He looked a little tired, but happy, and had brought a draft with him for five hundred and seventy-five dollars, which he explained was the total of his capital. Uncle Jim was overjoyed. They would start for Napa that very day, and conclude the purchase of the ranch; Uncle Jim's sprained foot was a sufficient reason for his giving up his present vocation, which he could also sell at a small profit. His domestic arrangements were very simple; there was nothing to take with him—there was everything to leave behind. And that afternoon, at sunset, the two reunited partners were seated on the deck of the Napa boat as she swung into the stream.

Uncle Billy was gazing over the railing with a look of abstracted relief towards the Golden Gate, where the sinking sun seemed to be drawing towards him in the ocean a golden stream that was forever pouring from the Bay and the three-hilled city beside it. What Uncle Billy was thinking of, or what the picture suggested to him, did not transpire; for Uncle Jim, who, emboldened by his holiday, was luxuriating in an evening paper, suddenly uttered a long-drawn whistle, and moved closer to his abstracted partner. "Look yer," he said, pointing to a paragraph he had evidently just read, "just you listen to this, and see if we ain't lucky, you and me, to be jest wot we air—trustin' to our own hard work—and not thinkin' o' 'strikes' and 'fortins.' Jest unbutton yer ears, Billy, while I reel off this yer thing I've jest struck in the paper, and see what d—d fools some men kin make o' themselves. And that theer reporter wot wrote it—must hev seed it reely!"

Uncle Jim cleared his throat, and holding the paper close to his eyes read aloud slowly:—

"'A scene of excitement that recalled the palmy days of '49 was witnessed last night at the Arcade Saloon. A stranger, who might have belonged to that reckless epoch, and who bore every evidence of being a successful Pike County miner out on a "spree," appeared at one of the tables with a negro coachman bearing two heavy bags of gold. Selecting a faro-bank as his base of operations, he began to bet heavily and with apparent recklessness, until his play excited the breathless attention of every one. In a few moments he had won a sum variously estimated at from eighty to a hundred thousand dollars. A rumor went round the room that it was a concerted attempt to "break the bank" rather than the drunken freak of a Western miner, dazzled by some successful strike. To this theory the man's careless and indifferent bearing towards his extraordinary gains lent great credence. The attempt, if such it was, however, was unsuccessful. After winning ten times in succession the luck turned, and the unfortunate "bucker" was cleared out not only of his gains, but of his original investment, which may be placed roughly at twenty thousand dollars. This extraordinary play was witnessed by a crowd of excited players, who were less impressed by even the magnitude of the stakes than the perfect sang-froid and recklessness of the player, who, it is said, at the close of the game tossed a twenty-dollar gold-piece to the banker and smilingly withdrew. The man was not recognized by any of the habitues of the place.'"

"There!" said Uncle Jim, as he hurriedly slurred over the French substantive at the close, "did ye ever see such God-forsaken foolishness?"

Uncle Billy lifted his abstracted eyes from the current, still pouring its unreturning gold into the sinking sun, and said, with a deprecatory smile, "Never!"

Nor even in the days of prosperity that visited the Great Wheat Ranch of "Fall and Foster" did he ever tell his secret to his partner.

SEE YUP

I don't suppose that his progenitors ever gave him that name, or, indeed, that it was a NAME at all; but it was currently believed that—as pronounced "See UP"—it meant that lifting of the outer angle of the eye common to the Mongolian. On the other hand, I had been told that there was an old Chinese custom of affixing some motto or legend, or even a sentence from Confucius, as a sign above their shops, and that two or more words, which might be merely equivalent to "Virtue is its own reward," or "Riches are deceitful," were believed by the simple Californian miner to be the name of the occupant himself. Howbeit, "See Yup" accepted it with the smiling patience of his race, and never went by any other. If one of the tunnelmen always addressed him as "Brigadier-General," "Judge," or "Commodore," it was understood to be only the American fondness for ironic title, and was never used except in personal conversation. In appearance he looked like any other Chinaman, wore the ordinary blue cotton blouse and white drawers of the Sampan coolie, and, in spite of the apparent cleanliness and freshness of these garments, always exhaled that singular medicated odor—half opium, half ginger—which we recognized as the common "Chinese smell."

Our first interview was characteristic of his patient quality. He had done my washing for several months, but I had never yet seen him. A meeting at last had become necessary to correct his impressions regarding "buttons"—which he had seemed to consider as mere excrescences, to be removed like superfluous dirt from soiled linen. I had expected him to call at my lodgings, but he had not yet made his appearance. One day, during the noontide recess of the little frontier school over which I presided, I returned rather early. Two or three of the smaller boys, who were loitering about the school-yard, disappeared with a certain guilty precipitation that I suspected for the moment, but which I presently dismissed from my mind. I passed through the empty school-room to my desk, sat down, and began to prepare the coming lessons. Presently I heard a faint sigh. Looking up, to my intense concern, I discovered a solitary Chinaman whom I had overlooked, sitting in a rigid attitude on a bench with his back to the window. He caught my eye and smiled sadly, but without moving.

"What are you doing here?" I asked sternly.

"Me washee shilts; me talkee 'buttons.'"

"Oh! you're See Yup, are you?"

"Allee same, John."

"Well, come here."

I continued my work, but he did not move.

"Come here, hang it! Don't you understand?"

"Me shabbee, 'comme yea.' But me no shabbee Mellican boy, who catchee me, allee same. YOU 'comme yea'—YOU shabbee?"

Indignant, but believing that the unfortunate man was still in fear of persecution from the mischievous urchins whom I had evidently just interrupted, I put down my pen and went over to him. Here I discovered, to my surprise and mortification, that his long pigtail was held hard and fast by the closed window behind him which the young rascals had shut down upon it, after having first noiselessly fished it outside with a hook and line. I apologized, opened the window, and released him. He did not complain, although he must have been fixed in that uncomfortable position for some minutes, but plunged at once into the business that brought him there.

"But WHY didn't you come to my lodgings?" I asked.

He smiled sadly but intelligently.

"Mishtel Bally [Mr. Barry, my landlord] he owce me five dollee fo washee, washee. He no payee me. He say he knock hellee outee me allee time I come for payee. So me no come HOUSEE, me come SCHOOLEE, Shabbee? Mellican boy no good, but not so big as Mellican man. No can hurtee Chinaman so much. Shabbee?"

Alas! I knew that this was mainly true. Mr. James Barry was an Irishman, whose finer religious feelings revolted against paying money to a heathen. I could not find it in my heart to say anything to See Yup about the buttons; indeed, I spoke in complimentary terms about the gloss of my shirts, and I think I meekly begged him to come again for my washing. When I went home I expostulated with Mr. Barry, but succeeded only in extracting from him the conviction that I was one of "thim black Republican fellys that worshiped naygurs." I had simply made an enemy of him. But I did not know that, at the same time, I had made a friend of See Yup!

I became aware of this a few days later, by the appearance on my desk of a small pot containing a specimen of camellia japonica in flower. I knew the school-children were in the habit of making presents to me in this furtive fashion,—leaving their own nosegays of wild flowers, or perhaps a cluster of roses from their parents' gardens,—but I also knew that this exotic was too rare to come from them. I remembered that See Yup had a Chinese taste for gardening, and a friend, another Chinaman, who kept a large nursery in the adjoining town. But my doubts were set at rest by the discovery of a small roll of red rice-paper containing my washing-bill, fastened to the camellia stalk. It was plain that this mingling of business and delicate gratitude was clearly See Yup's own idea. As the finest flower was the topmost one, I plucked it for wearing, when I found, to my astonishment, that it was simply wired to the stalk. This led me to look at the others, which I found also wired! More than that, they seemed to be an inferior flower, and exhaled that cold, earthy odor peculiar to the camellia, even, as I thought, to an excess. A closer examination resulted in the discovery that, with the exception of the first flower I had plucked, they were one and all ingeniously constructed of thin slices of potato, marvelously cut to imitate the vegetable waxiness and formality of the real flower. The work showed an infinite and almost pathetic patience in detail, yet strangely incommensurate with the result, admirable as it was. Nevertheless, this was also like See Yup. But whether he had tried to deceive me, or whether he only wished me to admire his skill, I could not say. And as his persecution by my scholars had left a balance of consideration in his favor, I sent him a warm note of thanks, and said nothing of my discovery.

As our acquaintance progressed, I became frequently the recipient of other small presents from him: a pot of preserves of a quality I could not purchase in shops, and whose contents in their crafty, gingery dissimulation so defied definition that I never knew whether they were animal, vegetable, or mineral; two or three hideous Chinese idols, "for luckee," and a diabolical fire-work with an irregular spasmodic activity that would sometimes be prolonged until the next morning. In return, I gave him some apparently hopeless oral lessons in English, and certain sentences to be copied, which he did with marvelous precision. I remember one instance when this peculiar faculty of imitation was disastrous in result. In setting him a copy, I had blurred a word which I promptly erased, and then traced the letters more distinctly over the scratched surface. To my surprise, See Yup triumphantly produced HIS copy with the erasion itself carefully imitated, and, in fact, much more neatly done than mine.

In our confidential intercourse, I never seemed to really get nearer to him. His sympathy and simplicity appeared like his flowers—to be a good-humored imitation of my own. I am satisfied that his particularly soulless laugh was not derived from any amusement he actually felt, yet I could not say it was forced. In his accurate imitations, I fancied he was only trying to evade any responsibility of his own. THAT devolved upon his taskmaster! In the attention he displayed when new ideas were presented to him, there was a slight condescension, as if he were looking down upon them from his three thousand years of history.

"Don't you think the electric telegraph wonderful?" I asked one day.

"Very good for Mellican man," he said, with his aimless laugh; "plenty makee him jump!"

I never could tell whether he had confounded it with electro-galvanism, or was only satirizing our American haste and feverishness. He was capable of either. For that matter, we knew that the Chinese themselves possessed some means of secretly and quickly communicating with one another. Any news of good or ill import to their race was quickly disseminated through the settlement before WE knew anything about it. An innocent basket of clothes from the wash, sent up from the river-bank, became in some way a library of information; a single slip of rice-paper, aimlessly fluttering in the dust of the road, had the mysterious effect of diverging a whole gang of coolie tramps away from our settlement.

When See Yup was not subject to the persecutions of the more ignorant and brutal he was always a source of amusement to all, and I cannot recall an instance when he was ever taken seriously. The miners found diversions even in his alleged frauds and trickeries, whether innocent or retaliatory, and were fond of relating with great gusto his evasion of the Foreign Miners' Tax. This was an oppressive measure aimed principally at the Chinese, who humbly worked the worn-out "tailings" of their Christian fellow miners. It was stated that See Yup, knowing the difficulty—already alluded to—of identifying any particular Chinaman by NAME, conceived the additional idea of confusing recognition by intensifying the monotonous facial expression. Having paid his tax himself to the collector, he at once passed the receipt to his fellows, so that the collector found himself confronted in different parts of the settlement with the receipt and the aimless laugh of, apparently, See Yup himself. Although we all knew that there were a dozen Chinamen or more at work at the mines, the collector never was able to collect the tax from more than TWO,—See Yup and one See Yin,—and so great was THEIR facial resemblance that the unfortunate official for a long time hugged himself with the conviction that he had made See Yup PAY TWICE, and withheld the money from the government! It is very probable that the Californian's recognition of the sanctity of a joke, and his belief that "cheating the government was only cheating himself," largely accounted for the sympathies of the rest of the miners.

But these sympathies were not always unanimous.

One evening I strolled into the bar-room of the principal saloon, which, so far as mere upholstery and comfort went, was also the principal house in the settlement. The first rains had commenced; the windows were open, for the influence of the southwest trades penetrated even this far-off mountain mining settlement, but, oddly enough, there was a fire in the large central stove, around which the miners had collected, with their steaming boots elevated on a projecting iron railing that encircled it. They were not attracted by the warmth, but the stove formed a social pivot for gossip, and suggested that mystic circle dear to the gregarious instinct. Yet they were decidedly a despondent group. For some moments the silence was only broken by a gasp, a sigh, a muttered oath, or an impatient change of position. There was nothing in the fortunes of the settlement, nor in their own individual affairs to suggest this gloom. The singular truth was that they were, one and all, suffering from the pangs of dyspepsia.

Incongruous as such a complaint might seem to their healthy environment,—their outdoor life, their daily exercise, the healing balsam of the mountain air, their enforced temperance in diet, and the absence of all enervating pleasures,—it was nevertheless the incontestable fact. Whether it was the result of the nervous, excitable temperament which had brought them together in this feverish hunt for gold; whether it was the quality of the tinned meats or half-cooked provisions they hastily bolted, begrudging the time it took to prepare and to consume them; whether they too often supplanted their meals by tobacco or whiskey, the singular physiological truth remained that these young, finely selected adventurers, living the lives of the natural, aboriginal man, and looking the picture of health and strength, actually suffered more from indigestion than the pampered dwellers of the cities. The quantity of "patent medicines," "bitters," "pills," "panaceas," and "lozenges" sold in the settlement almost exceeded the amount of the regular provisions whose effects they were supposed to correct. The sufferers eagerly scanned advertisements and placards. There were occasional "runs" on new "specifics," and general conversation eventually turned into a discussion of their respective merits. A certain childlike faith and trust in each new remedy was not the least distressing and pathetic of the symptoms of these grown-up, bearded men.

"Well, gentlemen," said Cyrus Parker, glancing around at his fellow sufferers, "ye kin talk of your patent medicines, and I've tackled 'em all, but only the other day I struck suthin' that I'm goin' to hang on to, you bet."

Every eye was turned moodily to the speaker, but no one said anything.

"And I didn't get it outer advertisements, nor off of circulars. I got it outer my head, just by solid thinking," continued Parker.

"What was it, Cy?" said one unsophisticated and inexperienced sufferer.

Instead of replying, Parker, like a true artist, knowing he had the ear of his audience, dramatically flashed a question upon them.

"Did you ever hear of a Chinaman having dyspepsy?"

"Never heard he had sabe enough to hev ANYTHING," said

a scorner.

"No, but DID ye?" insisted Parker.

"Well, no!" chorused the group. They were evidently struck with the fact.

"Of course you didn't," said Parker triumphantly. "'Cos they AIN'T. Well, gentlemen, it didn't seem to me the square thing that a pesky lot o' yellow-skinned heathens should be built different to a white man, and never know the tortur' that a Christian feels; and one day, arter dinner, when I was just a-lyin' flat down on the bank, squirmin', and clutching the short grass to keep from yellin', who should go by but that pizened See Yup, with a grin on his face.

"'Mellican man plenty playee to him Joss after eatin','' sez he; 'but Chinaman smellee punk, allee same, and no hab got.'"

"I knew the slimy cuss was just purtendin' he thought I was prayin' to my Joss, but I was that weak I hadn't stren'th, boys, to heave a rock at him. Yet it gave me an idea."

"What was it?" they asked eagerly.

"I went down to his shop the next day, when he was alone, and I was feeling mighty bad, and I got hold of his pigtail and I allowed I'd stuff it down his throat if he didn't tell me what he meant. Then he took a piece of punk and lit it, and put it under my nose, and, darn my skin, gentlemen, you migh'n't believe me, but in a minute I felt better, and after a whiff or two I was all right."

"Was it pow'ful strong, Cy?" asked the inexperienced one.

"No," said Parker, "and that's just what's got me. It was a sort o' dreamy, spicy smell, like a hot night. But as I couldn't go 'round 'mong you boys with a lighted piece o' punk in my hand, ez if I was settin' off Fourth of July firecrackers, I asked him if he couldn't fix me up suthin' in another shape that would be handier to use when I was took bad, and I'd reckon to pay him for it like ez I'd pay for any other patent medicine. So he fixed me up this."

He put his hand in his pocket, and drew out a small red paper which, when opened, disclosed a pink powder. It was gravely passed around the group.

"Why, it smells and tastes like ginger," said one.

"It is only ginger!" said another scornfully.

"Mebbe it is, and mebbe it isn't," returned Cy Parker stoutly. "Mebbe ut's only my fancy. But if it's the sort o' stuff to bring on that fancy, and that fancy CURES me, it's all the same. I've got about two dollars' worth o' that fancy or that ginger, and I'm going to stick to it. You hear me!" And he carefully put it back in his pocket.

At which criticisms and gibes broke forth. If he (Cy Parker), a white man, was going to "demean himself" by consulting a Chinese quack, he'd better buy up a lot o' idols and stand 'em up around his cabin. If he had that sort o' confidences with See Yup, he ought to go to work with him on his cheap tailings, and be fumigated all at the same time. If he'd been smoking an opium pipe, instead of smelling punk, he ought to be man enough to confess it. Yet it was noticeable that they were all very anxious to examine the packet again, but Cy Parker was alike indifferent to demand or entreaty.

A few days later I saw Abe Wynford, one of the party, coming out of See Yup's wash-house. He muttered something in passing about the infamous delay in sending home his washing, but did not linger long in conversation. The next day I met another miner AT the wash-house, but HE lingered so long on some trifling details that I finally left him there alone with See Yup. When I called upon Poker Jack of Shasta, there was a singular smell of incense in HIS cabin, which he attributed to the very resinous quality of the fir logs he was burning. I did not attempt to probe these mysteries by any direct appeal to See Yup himself: I respected his reticence; indeed, if I had not, I was quite satisfied that he would have lied to me. Enough that his wash-house was well patronized, and he was decidedly "getting on."

It might have been a month afterwards that Dr. Duchesne was setting a broken bone in the settlement, and after the operation was over, had strolled into the Palmetto Saloon. He was an old army surgeon, much respected and loved in the district, although perhaps a little feared for the honest roughness and military precision of his speech. After he had exchanged salutations with the miners in his usual hearty fashion, and accepted their invitation to drink, Cy Parker, with a certain affected carelessness which did not, however, conceal a singular hesitation in his speech, began:—

"I've been wantin' to ask ye a question, Doc,—a sort o' darned fool question, ye know,—nothing in the way of consultation, don't you see, though it's kin er in the way o' your purfeshun. Sabe?"

"Go on, Cy," said the doctor good-humoredly, "this is my dispensary hour."

"Oh! it ain't anything about symptoms, Doc, and there ain't anything the matter with me. It's only just to ask ye if ye happened to know anything about the medical practice of these yer Chinamen?"

"I don't know," said the doctor bluntly, "and I don't know ANYBODY who does."

There was a sudden silence in the bar, and the doctor, putting down his glass, continued with slight professional precision:—

"You see, the Chinese know nothing of anatomy from personal observation. Autopsies and dissection are against their superstitions, which declare the human body sacred, and are consequently never practiced."

There was a slight movement of inquiring interest among the party, and Cy Parker, after a meaning glance at the others, went on half aggressively, half apologetically:—

"In course, they ain't surgeons like you, Doc, but that don't keep them from having their own little medicines, just as dogs eat grass, you know. Now I want to put it to you, as a fa'r-minded man, if you mean ter say that, jest because those old women who sarve out yarbs and spring medicines in families don't know anything of anatomy, they ain't fit to give us their simple and nat'ral medicines?"

"But the Chinese medicines are not simple or natural," said the doctor coolly.

"Not simple?" echoed the party, closing round him.

"I don't mean to say," continued the doctor, glancing around at their eager, excited faces with an appearance of wonder, "that they are positively noxious, unless taken in large quantities, for they are not drugs at all, but I certainly should not call them 'simple.' Do YOU know what they principally are?"

"Well, no," said Parker cautiously, "perhaps not EXACTLY."

"Come a little closer, and I'll tell you."

Not only Parker's head but the others were bent over the counter. Dr. Duchesne uttered a few words in a tone inaudible to the rest of the company. There was a profound silence, broken at last by Abe Wynford's voice:—

"Ye kin pour me out about three fingers o' whiskey, Barkeep. I'll take it straight."

"Same to me," said the others.

The men gulped down their liquor; two of them quietly passed out. The doctor wiped his lips, buttoned his coat, and began to draw on his riding-gloves.

"I've heerd," said Poker Jack of Shasta, with a faint smile on his white face, as he toyed with the last drops of liquor in his glass, "that the darned fools sometimes smell punk as a medicine, eh?"

"Yes, THAT'S comparatively decent," said the doctor reflectively. "It's only sawdust mixed with a little gum and formic acid."

"Formic acid? Wot's that?"

"A very peculiar acid secreted by ants. It is supposed to be used by them offensively in warfare—just as the skunk, eh?"

But Poker Jack of Shasta had hurriedly declared that he wanted to speak to a man who was passing, and had disappeared. The doctor walked to the door, mounted his horse, and rode away. I noticed, however, that there was a slight smile on his bronzed, impassive face. This led me to wonder if he was entirely ignorant of the purpose for which he had been questioned, and the effect of his information. I was confirmed in the belief by the remarkable circumstances that nothing more was said of it; the incident seemed to have terminated there, and the victims made no attempt to revenge themselves on See Yup. That they had one and all, secretly and unknown to one another, patronized him, there was no doubt; but, at the same time, as they evidently were not sure that Dr. Duchesne had not hoaxed them in regard to the quality of See Yup's medicines, they knew that an attack on the unfortunate Chinaman would in either case reveal their secret and expose them to the ridicule of their brother miners. So the matter dropped, and See Yup remained master of the situation.

Meantime he was prospering. The coolie gang he worked on the river, when not engaged in washing clothes, were "picking over" the "tailings," or refuse of gravel, left on abandoned claims by successful miners. As there was no more expense attending this than in stone-breaking or rag-picking, and the feeding of the coolies, which was ridiculously cheap, there was no doubt that See Yup was reaping a fair weekly return from it; but, as he sent his receipts to San Francisco through coolie managers, after the Chinese custom, and did not use the regular Express Company, there was no way of ascertaining the amount. Again, neither See Yup nor his fellow countrymen ever appeared to have any money about them. In ruder times and more reckless camps, raids were often made by ruffians on their cabins or their traveling gangs, but never with any pecuniary result. This condition, however, it seemed was destined to change.

One Saturday See Yup walked into Wells, Fargo & Co.'s

Express office with a package of gold-dust, which, when duly weighed, was valued at five hundred dollars. It was consigned to a Chinese company in San Francisco. When the clerk handed See Yup a receipt, he remarked casually:—

"Washing seems to pay, See Yup."

"Washee velly good pay. You wantee washee, John?" said See Yup eagerly.

"No, no," said the clerk, with a laugh. "I was only thinking five hundred dollars would represent the washing of a good many shirts."

"No leplesent washee shirts at all! Catchee gold-dust when washee tailings. Shabbee?"

The clerk DID "shabbee," and lifted his eyebrows. The next Saturday See Yup appeared with another package, worth about four hundred dollars, directed to the same consignee.

"Didn't pan out quite so rich this week, eh?" said the clerk engagingly.

"No," returned See Yup impassively; "next time he payee more."

When the third Saturday came, with the appearance of See Yup and four hundred and fifty dollars' worth of gold-dust, the clerk felt he was no longer bound to keep the secret. He communicated it to others, and in twenty-four hours the whole settlement knew that See Yup's coolie company were taking out an average of four hundred dollars per week from the refuse and tailings of the old abandoned Palmetto claim!

The astonishment of the settlement was profound. In earlier

days jealousy and indignation at the success of these degraded heathens might have taken a more active and aggressive shape, and it would have fared ill with See Yup and his companions. But the settlement had become more prosperous and law-abiding; there were one or two Eastern families and some foreign capital already there, and its jealousy and indignation were restricted to severe investigation and legal criticism. Fortunately for See Yup, it was an old-established mining law that an abandoned claim and its tailings became the property of whoever chose to work it. But it was alleged that See Yup's company had in reality "struck a lead,"—discovered a hitherto unknown vein or original deposit of gold, not worked by the previous company, and having failed legally to declare it by preemption and public registry, in their foolish desire for secrecy, had thus forfeited their right to the property. A surveillance of their working, however, did not establish this theory; the gold that See Yup had sent away was of the kind that might have been found in the tailings overlooked by the late Palmetto owners. Yet it was a very large yield for mere refuse.

"Them Palmetto boys were mighty keerless after they'd made their big 'strike' and got to work on the vein, and I reckon they threw a lot of gold away," said Cy Parker, who remembered their large-handed recklessness in the "flush days." "On'y that WE didn't think it was white man's work to rake over another man's leavin's, we might hev had what them derned Chinamen hev dropped into. Tell ye what, boys, we've been a little too 'high and mighty,' and we'll hev to climb down."

At last the excitement reached its climax, and diplomacy was employed to effect what neither intimidation nor espionage could secure. Under the pretense of desiring to buy out See Yup's company, a select committee of the miners was permitted to examine the property and its workings. They found the great bank of stones and gravel, representing the cast-out debris of the old claim, occupied by See Yup and four or five plodding automatic coolies. At the end of two hours the committee returned to the saloon bursting with excitement. They spoke under their breath, but enough was gathered to satisfy the curious crowd that See Yup's pile of tailings was rich beyond their expectations. The committee had seen with their own eyes gold taken out of the sand and gravel to the amount of twenty dollars in the two short hours of their examination. And the work had been performed in the stupidest, clumsiest, yet PATIENT Chinese way. What might not white men do with better appointed machinery! A syndicate was at once formed. See Yup was offered twenty thousand dollars if he would sell out and put the syndicate in possession of the claim in twenty-four hours. The Chinaman received the offer stolidly. As he seemed inclined to hesitate, I am grieved to say that it was intimated to him that if he declined he might be subject to embarrassing and expensive legal proceedings to prove his property, and that companies would be formed to "prospect" the ground on either side of his heap of tailings. See Yup at last consented, with the proviso that the money should be paid in gold into the hands of a Chinese agent in San Francisco on the day of the delivery of the claim. The syndicate made no opposition to this characteristic precaution of the Chinaman. It was like them not to travel with money, and the implied uncomplimentary suspicion of danger from the community was overlooked. See Yup departed the day that the syndicate took possession. He came to see me before he went. I congratulated him upon his good fortune; at the same time, I was embarrassed by the conviction that he was unfairly forced into a sale of his property at a figure far below its real value.

I think differently now.

At the end of the week it was said that the new company cleared up about three hundred dollars. This was not so much as the community had expected, but the syndicate was apparently satisfied, and the new machinery was put up. At the end of the next week the syndicate were silent as to their returns. One of them made a hurried visit to San Francisco. It was said that he was unable to see either See Yup or the agent to whom the money was paid. It was also noticed that there was no Chinaman remaining in the settlement. Then the fatal secret was out.

The heap of tailings had probably never yielded the See Yup company more than twenty dollars a week, the ordinary wage of such a company. See Yup had conceived the brilliant idea of "booming" it on a borrowed capital of five hundred dollars in gold-dust, which he OPENLY transmitted by express to his confederate and creditor in San Francisco, who in turn SECRETLY sent it back to See Yup by coolie messengers, to be again openly transmitted to San Francisco. The package of gold-dust was thus passed backwards and forwards between debtor and creditor, to the grave edification of the Express Company and the fatal curiosity of the settlement. When the syndicate had gorged the bait thus thrown out, See Yup, on the day the self-invited committee inspected the claim, promptly "salted" the tailings by CONSCIENTIOUSLY DISTRIBUTING THE GOLD-DUST OVER IT so deftly that it appeared to be its natural composition and yield.

I have only to bid farewell to See Yup, and close this reminiscence of a misunderstood man, by adding the opinion of an eminent jurist in San Francisco, to whom the facts were submitted: "So clever was this alleged fraud, that it is extremely doubtful if an action would lie against See Yup in the premises, there being no legal evidence of the 'salting,' and none whatever of his actual allegation that the gold-dust was the ORDINARY yield of the tailings, that implication resting entirely with the committee who examined it under false pretense, and who subsequently forced the sale by intimidation."

THE DESBOROUGH CONNECTIONS

"Then it isn't a question of property or next of kin?" said the consul.

"Lord! no," said the lady vivaciously. "Why, goodness me! I reckon old Desborough could, at any time before he died, have 'bought up' or 'bought out' the whole lot of his relatives on this side of the big pond, no matter what they were worth. No, it's only a matter of curiosity and just sociableness."

The American consul at St. Kentigorn felt much relieved. He had feared it was only the old story of delusive quests for imaginary estates and impossible inheritances which he had confronted so often in nervous wan-eyed enthusiasts and obstreperous claimants from his own land. Certainly there was no suggestion of this in the richly dressed and be-diamonded matron before him, nor in her pretty daughter, charming in a Paris frock, alive with the consciousness of beauty and admiration, and yet a little ennuye from gratified indulgence. He knew the mother to be the wealthy widow of a New York millionaire, that she was traveling for pleasure in Europe, and a chance meeting with her at dinner a few nights before had led to this half-capricious, half-confidential appointment at the consulate.

"No," continued Mrs. Desborough; "Mr. Desborough came

to America, when a small boy, with an uncle who died some years ago. Mr. Desborough never seemed to hanker much after his English relatives as long as I knew him, but now that I and Sadie are over here, why we guessed we might look 'em up and sort of sample 'em! 'Desborough' 's rather a good name," added the lady, with a complacency that, however, had a suggestion of query in it.

"Yes," said the consul; "from the French, I fancy."

"Mr. Desborough was English—very English," corrected the lady.

"I mean it may be an old Norman name," said the consul.

"Norman's good enough for ME," said the daughter, reflecting. "We'll just settle it as Norman. I never thought about that DES."

"Only you may find it called 'Debborough' here, and spelt so," said the consul, smiling.

Miss Desborough lifted her pretty shoulders and made a charming grimace. "Then we won't acknowledge 'em. No Debborough for me!"

"You might put an advertisement in the papers, like the 'next of kin' notice, intimating, in the regular way, that they would 'hear of something to their advantage'—as they certainly would," continued the consul, with a bow. "It would be such a refreshing change to the kind of thing I'm accustomed to, don't you know—this idea of one of my countrywomen coming over just to benefit English relatives! By Jove! I wouldn't mind undertaking the whole thing for you—it's such a novelty." He was quite carried away with the idea.

But the two ladies were far from participating in this joyous outlook. "No," said Mrs. Desborough promptly, "that wouldn't do. You see," she went on with superb frankness, "that would be just giving ourselves away, and saying who WE were before we found out what THEY were like. Mr. Desborough was all right in HIS way, but we don't know anything about his FOLKS! We ain't here on a mission to improve the Desboroughs, nor to gather in any 'lost tribes.'"

It was evident that, in spite of the humor of the situation and the levity of the ladies, there was a characteristic national practicalness about them, and the consul, with a sigh, at last gave the address of one or two responsible experts in genealogical inquiry, as he had often done before. He felt it was impossible to offer any advice to ladies as thoroughly capable of managing their own affairs as his fair country-women, yet he was not without some curiosity to know the result of their practical sentimental quest. That he should ever hear of them again he doubted. He knew that after their first loneliness had worn off in their gregarious gathering at a London hotel they were not likely to consort with their own country people, who indeed were apt to fight shy of one another, and even to indulge in invidious criticism of one another when admitted in that society to which they were all equally strangers. So he took leave of them on their way back to London with the belief that their acquaintance terminated with that brief incident. But he was mistaken.

In the year following he was spending his autumn vacation at a country house. It was an historic house, and had always struck him as being—even in that country of historic seats— a singular example of the vicissitudes of English manorial estates and the mutations of its lords. His host in his prime had been recalled from foreign service to unexpectedly succeed to an uncle's title and estate. That estate, however, had come into the possession of the uncle only through his marriage with the daughter of an old family whose portraits still looked down from the walls upon the youngest and alien branch. There were likenesses, effigies, memorials, and reminiscences of still older families who had occupied it through forfeiture by war or the favoritism of kings, and in its stately cloisters and ruined chapel was still felt the dead hand of its evicted religious founders, which could not be shaken off.

It was this strange individuality that affected all who saw it. For, however changed were those within its walls, whoever were its inheritors or inhabiters, Scrooby Priory never changed nor altered its own character. However incongruous or ill-assorted the portraits that looked from its walls,—so ill met that they might have flown at one another's throats in the long nights when the family were away,—the great house itself was independent of them all. The be-wigged, be-laced, and be-furbelowed of one day's gathering, the round-headed, steel-fronted, and prim-kerchiefed congregation of another day, and even the black-coated, bare-armed, and bare-shouldered assemblage of to-day had no effect on the austerities of the Priory. Modern houses might show the tastes and prepossessions of their dwellers, might have caught some passing trick of the hour, or have recorded the augmented fortunes or luxuriousness of the owner, but Scrooby Priory never! No one had dared even to disturb its outer rigid integrity; the breaches of time and siege were left untouched. It held its calm indifferent sway over all who passed its low-arched portals, and the consul was fain to believe that he—a foreign visitor—was no more alien to the house than its present owner.

"I'm expecting a very charming compatriot of yours to-morrow," said Lord Beverdale as they drove from the station together. "You must tell me what to show her."

"I should think any countrywoman of mine would be quite satisfied with the Priory," said the consul, glancing thoughtfully towards the pile dimly seen through the park.

"I shouldn't like her to be bored here," continued Beverdale. "Algy met her at Rome, where she was occupying a palace with her mother—they're very rich, you know. He found she was staying with Lady Minever at Hedham Towers, and I went over and invited her with a little party. She's a Miss Desborough."

The consul gave a slight start, and was aware that Beverdale was looking at him.

"Perhaps you know her?" said Beverdale.

"Just enough to agree with you that she is charming," said the consul. "I dined with them, and saw them at the consulate."

"Oh yes; I always forget you are a consul. Then, of course, you know all about them. I suppose they're very rich, and in society over there?" said Beverdale in a voice that was quite animated.

It was on the consul's lips to say that the late Mr. Desborough was an Englishman, and even to speak playfully of their proposed quest, but a sudden instinct withheld him. After all, perhaps it was only a caprice, or idea, they had forgotten,—perhaps, who knows?—that they were already ashamed of. They had evidently "got on" in English society, if that was their real intent, and doubtless Miss Desborough, by this time, was quite as content with the chance of becoming related to the Earl of Beverdale, through his son and heir, Algernon, as if they had found a real Lord Desborough among their own relatives. The consul knew that Lord Beverdale was not a rich man, that like most men of old family he was not a slave to class prejudice; indeed, the consul had seen very few noblemen off the stage or out of the pages of a novel who were. So he said, with a slight affectation of authority, that there was as little doubt of the young lady's wealth as there was of her personal attractions.

They were nearing the house through a long avenue of chestnuts whose variegated leaves were already beginning to strew the ground beneath, and they could see the vista open upon the mullioned windows of the Priory, lighted up by the yellow October sunshine. In that sunshine stood a tall, clean-limbed young fellow, dressed in a shooting-suit, whom the consul recognized at once as Lord Algernon, the son of his companion. As if to accent the graces of this vision of youth and vigor, near him, in the shadow, an old man had halted, hat in hand, still holding the rake with which he had been gathering the dead leaves in the avenue; his back bent, partly with years, partly with the obeisance of a servitor. There was something so marked in this contrast, in this old man standing in the shadow of the fading year, himself as dried and withered as the leaves he was raking, yet pausing to make his reverence to this passing sunshine of youth and prosperity in the presence of his coming master, that the consul, as they swept by, looked after him with a stirring of pain.

"Rather an old man to be still at work," said the consul.

Beverdale laughed. "You must not let him hear you say so; he considers himself quite as fit as any younger man in the place, and, by Jove! though he's nearly eighty, I'm inclined to believe it. He's not one of our people, however; he comes from the village, and is taken on at odd times, partly to please himself. His great aim is to be independent of his children,—he has a granddaughter who is one of the maids at the Priory,—and to keep himself out of the workhouse. He does not come from these parts—somewhere farther north, I fancy. But he's a tough lot, and has a deal of work in him yet."

"Seems to be going a bit stale lately," said Lord Algernon, "and I think is getting a little queer in his head. He has a trick of stopping and staring straight ahead, at times, when he seems to go off for a minute or two. There!" continued the young man, with a light laugh. "I say! he's doing it now!" They both turned quickly and gazed at the bent figure—not fifty yards away—standing in exactly the same attitude as before. But, even as they gazed, he slowly lifted his rake and began his monotonous work again.

At Scrooby Priory, the consul found that the fame of his fair countrywoman had indeed preceded her, and that the other guests were quite as anxious to see Miss Desborough as he was. One of them had already met her in London; another knew her as one of the house party at the Duke of Northforeland's, where she had been a central figure. Some of her naive sallies and frank criticisms were repeated with great unction by the gentlemen, and with some slight trepidation and a "fearful joy" by the ladies. He was more than ever convinced that mother and daughter had forgotten their lineal Desboroughs, and he resolved to leave any allusion to it to the young lady herself.

She, however, availed herself of that privilege the evening after her arrival. "Who'd have thought of meeting YOU here?" she said, sweeping her skirts away to make room for him on a sofa. "It's a coon's age since I saw you—not since you gave us that letter to those genealogical gentlemen in London."

The consul hoped that it had proved successful.

"Yes, but maw guessed we didn't care to go back to Hengist and Horsa, and when they let loose a lot of 'Debboroughs' and 'Daybrooks' upon us, maw kicked! We've got a drawing ten yards long, that looks like a sour apple tree, with lots of Desboroughs hanging up on the branches like last year's pippins, and I guess about as worm-eaten. We took that well enough, but when it came to giving us a map of straight lines and dashes with names written under them like an old Morse telegraph slip, struck by lightning, then maw and I guessed that it made us tired.

"You know," she went on, opening her clear gray eyes on the consul, with a characteristic flash of shrewd good sense through her quaint humor, "we never reckoned where this thing would land us, and we found we were paying a hundred pounds, not only for the Desboroughs, but all the people they'd MARRIED, and their CHILDREN, and children's children, and there were a lot of outsiders we'd never heard of, nor wanted to hear of. Maw once thought she'd got on the trail of a Plantagenet, and followed it keen, until she found she had been reading the dreadful thing upside down. Then we concluded we wouldn't take any more stock in the family until it had risen."

During this speech the consul could not help noticing that, although her attitude was playfully confidential to him, her voice really was pitched high enough to reach the ears of smaller groups around her, who were not only following her with the intensest admiration, but had shamelessly abandoned their own conversation, and had even faced towards her. Was she really posing in her naivete? There was a certain mischievous, even aggressive, consciousness in her pretty eyelids. Then she suddenly dropped both eyes and voice, and said to the consul in a genuine aside, "I like this sort of thing much better."

The consul looked puzzled. "What sort of thing?"

"Why, all these swell people, don't you see? those pictures on the walls! this elegant room! everything that has come down from the past, all ready and settled for you, you know—ages ago! Something you haven't to pick up for yourself and worry over."

But here the consul pointed out that the place itself was not "ancestral" as regarded the present earl, and that even the original title of his predecessors had passed away from it. "In fact, it came into the family by one of those 'outsiders' you deprecate. But I dare say you'd find the place quite as comfortable with Lord Beverdale for a host as you would if you had found out he were a cousin," he added.

"Better," said the young lady frankly.

"I suppose your mother participates in these preferences?" said the consul, with a smile.

"No," said Miss Desborough, with the same frankness, "I think maw's rather cut up at not finding a Desborough. She was invited down here, but SHE'S rather independent, you know, so she allowed I could take care of myself, while she went off to stay with the old Dowager Lady Mistowe, who thinks maw a very proper womanly person. I made maw mad by telling her that's just what old Lady Mistowe would say of her cook—for I can't stand these people's patronage. However, I shouldn't wonder if I was invited here as a 'most original person.'"

But here Lord Algernon came up to implore her to sing them one of "those plantation songs;" and Miss Desborough, with scarcely a change of voice or manner, allowed herself to be led to the piano. The consul had little chance to speak with her again, but he saw enough that evening to convince him not only that Lord Algernon was very much in love with her, but that the fact had been equally and complacently accepted by the family and guests. That her present visit was only an opportunity for a formal engagement was clear to every woman in the house—not excepting, I fear, even the fair subject of gossip herself. Yet she seemed so unconcerned and self-contained that the consul wondered if she really cared for Lord Algernon. And having thus wondered, he came to the conclusion that it didn't much matter, for the happiness of so practically organized a young lady, if she loved him or not.

It is highly probable that Miss Sadie Desborough had not even gone so far as to ask herself that question. She awoke the next morning with a sense of easy victory and calm satisfaction that had, however, none of the transports of affection. Her taste was satisfied by the love of a handsome young fellow,—a typical Englishman,—who, if not exactly original or ideal, was, she felt, of an universally accepted, "hall-marked" standard, the legitimate outcome of a highly ordered, carefully guarded civilization, whose repose was the absence of struggle or ambition; a man whose regular features were not yet differentiated from the rest of his class by any of those disturbing lines which people call character. Everything was made ready for her, without care or preparation; she had not even an ideal to realize or to modify. She could slip without any jar or dislocation into this life which was just saved from self-indulgence and sybaritic luxury by certain conventional rules of activity and the occupation of amusement which, as obligations of her position, even appeared to suggest the novel aspect of a DUTY! She could accept all this without the sense of being an intruder in an unbroken lineage—thanks to the consul's account of the Beverdales' inheritance. She already pictured herself as the mistress of this fair domain, the custodian of its treasures and traditions, and the dispenser of its hospitalities, but—as she conscientiously believed—without pride or vanity, in her position; only an intense and thoughtful appreciation of it. Nor did she dream of ever displaying it ostentatiously before her less fortunate fellow countrywomen; on the contrary, she looked forward to their possible criticism of her casting off all transatlantic ties with an uneasy consciousness that was perhaps her nearest approach to patriotism. Yet, again, she reasoned that, as her father was an Englishman, she was only returning to her old home. As to her mother, she had already comforted herself by noticing certain discrepancies in that lady's temperament, which led her to believe that she herself alone inherited her father's nature—for her mother was, of course, distinctly American! So little conscious was she of any possible snobbishness in this belief, that in her superb naivete she would have argued the point with the consul, and employed a wit and dialect that were purely American.

She had slipped out of the Priory early that morning that she might enjoy alone, unattended and uniceroned, the aspect of that vast estate which might be hers for the mere accepting. Perhaps there was some instinct of delicacy in her avoiding Lord Algernon that morning; not wishing, as she herself might have frankly put it, "to take stock" of his inheritance in his presence. As she passed into the garden through the low postern door, she turned to look along the stretching facade of the main building, with the high stained windows of its banqueting-hall and the state chamber where a king had slept. Even in that crisp October air, and with the green of its ivied battlements against the gold of the distant wood, it seemed to lie in the languid repose of an eternal summer. She hurried on down the other terrace into the Italian garden, a quaint survival of past grandeur, passed the great orangery and numerous conservatories, making a crystal hamlet in themselves—seeing everywhere the same luxury. But it was a luxury that she fancied was redeemed from the vulgarity of ostentation by the long custom of years and generations, so unlike the millionaire palaces of her own land; and, in her enthusiasm, she even fancied it was further sanctified by the grim monastic founders who had once been content with bread and pulse in the crumbling and dismantled refectory. In the plenitude of her feelings she felt a slight recognition of some beneficent being who had rolled this golden apple at her feet, and felt as if she really should like to "do good" in her sphere.

It so chanced that, passing through a small gate in the park, she saw walking, a little ahead of her, a young girl whom she at once recognized as a Miss Amelyn, one of the guests of the evening before. Miss Desborough remembered that she played the accompaniment of one or two songs upon the piano, and had even executed a long solo during the general conversation, without attention from the others, and apparently with little irritation to herself, subsiding afterwards into an armchair, quite on the fringe of other people's conversation. She had been called "my dear" by one or two dowagers, and by her Christian name by the earl, and had a way of impalpably melting out of sight at times. These trifles led Miss Desborough to conclude that she was some kind of dependent or poor relation. Here was an opportunity to begin her work of "doing good." She quickened her pace and overtook Miss Amelyn.

"Let me walk with you," she said graciously.

The young English girl smiled assent, but looked her surprise at seeing the cynosure of last night's eyes unattended.

"Oh," said Sadie, answering the mute query, "I didn't want to be 'shown round' by anybody, and I'm not going to bore YOU with asking to see sights either. We'll just walk together; wherever YOU'RE going is good enough for me."

"I'm going as far as the village," said Miss Amelyn, looking down doubtfully at Sadie's smart French shoes—"if you care to walk so far."

Sadie noticed that her companion was more solidly booted, and that her straight, short skirts, although less stylish than her own, had a certain character, better fitted to the freer outdoor life of the country. But she only said, however, "The village will do," and gayly took her companion's arm.

"But I'm afraid you'll find it very uninteresting, for I am going to visit some poor cottages," persisted Miss Amelyn, with a certain timid ingenuousness of manner which, however, was as distinct as Miss Desborough's bolder frankness. "I promised the rector's daughter to take her place to-day."

"And I feel as if I was ready to pour oil and wine to any extent," said Miss Desborough, "so come along!"

Miss Amelyn laughed, and yet glanced around her timidly, as if she thought that Miss Desborough ought to have a larger and more important audience. Then she continued more confidentially and boldly, "But it isn't at all like 'slumming,' you know. These poor people here are not very bad, and are not at all extraordinary."

"Never mind," said Sadie, hurrying her along. After a pause she went on, "You know the Priory very well, I guess?"

"I lived there when I was a little girl, with my aunt, the Dowager Lady Beverdale," said Miss Amelyn. "When my cousin Fred, who was the young heir, died, and the present Lord Beverdale succeeded,—HE never expected it, you know, for there were two lives, his two elder brothers, besides poor Fred's, between, but they both died,—we went to live in the Dower House."

"The Dower House?" repeated Sadie.

"Yes, Lady Beverdale's separate property."

"But I thought all this property—the Priory—came into the family through HER."

"It did—this was the Amelyns' place; but the oldest son or nearest male heir always succeeds to the property and title."

"Do you mean to say that the present Lord Beverdale turned that old lady out?"

Miss Amelyn looked shocked. "I mean to say," she said gravely, "Lady Beverdale would have had to go when her own son became of age, had he lived." She paused, and then said timidly, "Isn't it that way in America?"

"Dear no!" Miss Desborough had a faint recollection that there was something in the Constitution or the Declaration of Independence against primogeniture. "No! the men haven't it ALL their own way THERE—not much!"

Miss Amelyn looked as if she did not care to discuss this problem. After a few moments Sadie continued, "You and Lord Algernon are pretty old friends, I guess?"

"No," replied Miss Amelyn. "He came once or twice to the Priory for the holidays, when he was quite a boy at Marlborough—for the family weren't very well off, and his father was in India. He was a very shy boy, and of course no one ever thought of him succeeding."

Miss Desborough felt half inclined to be pleased with this,

and yet half inclined to resent this possible snubbing of her future husband. But they were nearing the village, and Miss Amelyn turned the conversation to the object of her visit. It was a new village—an unhandsome village, for all that it stood near one of the gates of the park. It had been given over to some mines that were still worked in its vicinity, and to the railway, which the uncle of the present earl had resisted; but the railway had triumphed, and the station for Scrooby Priory was there. There was a grim church, of a blackened or weather-beaten stone, on the hill, with a few grim Amelyns reposing cross-legged in the chancel, but the character of the village was as different from the Priory as if it were in another county. They stopped at the rectory, where Miss Amelyn provided herself with certain doles and gifts, which the American girl would have augmented with a five-pound note but for Miss Amelyn's horrified concern. "As many shillings would do, and they would be as grateful," she said. "More they wouldn't understand."

"Then keep it, and dole it out as you like," said Sadie quickly.

"But I don't think that—that Lord Beverdale would quite approve," hesitated Miss Amelyn.

The pretty brow of her companion knit, and her gray eyes flashed vivaciously. "What has HE to do with it?" she said pertly; "besides, you say these are not HIS poor. Take that five-pound note—or—I'll DOUBLE it, get it changed into sovereigns at the station, and hand 'em round to every man, woman, and child."

Miss Amelyn hesitated. The American girl looked capable of doing what she said; perhaps it was a national way of almsgiving! She took the note, with the mental reservation of making a full confession to the rector and Lord Beverdale.

She was right in saying that the poor of Scrooby village were not interesting. There was very little squalor or degradation; their poverty seemed not a descent, but a condition to which they had been born; the faces which Sadie saw were dulled and apathetic rather than sullen or rebellious; they stood up when Miss Amelyn entered, paying HER the deference, but taking little note of the pretty butterfly who was with her, or rather submitting to her frank curiosity with that dull consent of the poor, as if they had lost even the sense of privacy, or a right to respect. It seemed to the American girl that their poverty was more indicated by what they were SATISFIED with than what she thought they MISSED. It is to be feared that this did not add to Sadie's sympathy; all the beggars she had seen in America wanted all they could get, and she felt as if she were confronted with an inferior animal.

"There's a wonderful old man lives here," said Miss Amelyn, as they halted before a stone and thatch cottage quite on the outskirts of the village. "We can't call him one of our poor, for he still works, although over eighty, and it's his pride to keep out of the poorhouse, and, as he calls it, 'off' the hands of his granddaughters. But we manage to do something for THEM, and we hope he profits by it. One of them is at the Priory; they're trying to make a maid of her, but her queer accent—they're from the north—is against her with the servants. I am afraid we won't see old Debs, for he's at work again to-day, though the doctor has warned him."

"Debs! What a funny name!"

"Yes, but as many of these people cannot read or write, the name is carried by the ear, and not always correctly. Some of the railway navvies, who come from the north as he does, call him 'Debbers.'"

They were obliged to descend into the cottage, which was so

low that it seemed to have sunk into the earth until its drooping eaves of thatch mingled with the straw heap beside it. Debs was not at home. But his granddaughter was there, who, after a preliminary "bob," continued the stirring of the pot before the fire in tentative silence.

"I am sorry to find that your grandfather has gone to work again in spite of the doctor's orders," said Miss Amelyn.

The girl continued to stir the pot, and then said without looking up, but as if also continuing a train of aggressive thoughts with her occupation: "Eay, but 'e's so set oop in 'issen 'ee doan't take orders from nobbut—leastways doctor. Moinds 'em now moor nor a floy. Says 'ee knaws there nowt wrong wi' 'is 'eart. Mout be roight—how'siver, sarten sewer, 'is 'EAD'S a' in a muddle! Toims 'ee goes off stamrin' and starin' at nowt, as if 'ee a'nt a n'aporth o' sense. How'siver I be doing my duty by 'em—and 'ere's 'is porritch when a' cooms—'gin a' be sick or maad."

What the American understood of the girl's speech and manner struck her as having very little sympathy with either her aged relative or her present visitor. And there was a certain dogged selfish independence about her that Miss Desborough half liked and half resented. However, Miss Amelyn did not seem to notice it, and, after leaving a bottle of port for the grandfather, she took her leave and led Sadie away. As they passed into the village a carriage, returning to the Priory, filled with their fellow guests, dashed by, but was instantly pulled up at a word from Lord Algernon, who leaped from the vehicle, hat in hand, and implored the fair truant and her companion to join them.

"We're just making a tour around Windover Hill, and back to luncheon," he said, with a rising color. "We missed you awfully! If we had known you were so keen on 'good works,' and so early at it, by Jove! we'd have got up a 'slummin' party,' and all joined!"

"And you haven't seen half," said Lord Beverdale from the box. "Miss Amelyn's too partial to the village. There's an old drunken retired poacher somewhere in a hut in Crawley Woods, whom it's death to approach, except with a large party. There's malignant diphtheria over at the South Farm, eight down with measles at the keeper's, and an old woman who has been bedridden for years."

But Miss Desborough was adamant, though sparkling. She thanked him, but said she had just seen an old woman "who had been lying in bed for twenty years, and hadn't spoken the truth once!" She proposed "going outside of Lord Beverdale's own preserves of grain-fed poor," and starting up her own game. She would return in time for luncheon—if she could; if not, she "should annex the gruel of the first kind incapable she met."

Yet, actually, she was far from displeased at being accidentally discovered by these people while following out her capricious whim of the morning. One or two elder ladies, who had fought shy of her frocks and her frankness the evening before, were quite touched now by this butterfly who was willing to forego the sunlight of society, and soil her pretty wings on the haunts of the impoverished, with only a single companion,—of her own sex!—and smiled approvingly. And in her present state of mind, remembering her companion's timid attitude towards Lord Beverdale's opinions, she was not above administering this slight snub to him in her presence.

When they had driven away, with many regrets, Miss Amelyn was deeply concerned. "I am afraid," she said, with timid conscientiousness, "I have kept you from going with them. And you must be bored with what you have seen, I know. I don't believe you really care one bit for it—and you are only doing it to please me."

"Trot out the rest of your show," said Sadie promptly, "and we'll wind up by lunching with the rector."

"He'd be too delighted," said Miss Amelyn, with disaster written all over her girlish, truthful face, "but—but—you know—it really wouldn't be quite right to Lord Beverdale. You're his principal guest—you know, and—they'd think I had taken you off."

"Well," said Miss Desborough impetuously, "what's the matter with that inn—the Red Lion? We can get a sandwich there, I guess. I'm not VERY hungry."

Miss Amelyn looked horrified for a moment, and then laughed; but immediately became concerned again. "No! listen to me, REALLY now! Let me finish my round alone! You'll have ample time if you go NOW to reach the Priory for luncheon. Do, please! It would be ever so much better for everybody. I feel quite guilty as it is, and I suppose I am already in Lord Beverdale's black books."

The trouble in the young girl's face was unmistakable, and as it suited Miss Desborough's purpose just as well to show her independence by returning, as she had set out, alone, she consented to go. Miss Amelyn showed her a short cut across the park, and they separated—to meet at dinner. In this brief fellowship, the American girl had kept a certain supremacy and half-fascination over the English girl, even while she was conscious of an invincible character in Miss Amelyn entirely different from and superior to her own. Certainly there was a difference in the two peoples. Why else this inherited conscientious reverence for Lord Beverdale's position, shown by Miss Amelyn, which she, an American alive to its practical benefits, could not understand? Would Miss Amelyn and Lord Algernon have made a better match? The thought irritated her, even while she knew that she herself possessed the young man's affections, the power to marry him, and, as she believed, kept her own independence in the matter.

As she entered the iron gates at the lower end of the park, and glanced at the interwoven cipher and crest of the Amelyns still above, she was conscious that the wind was blowing more chill, and that a few clouds had gathered. As she walked on down the long winding avenue, the sky became overcast, and, in one of those strange contrasts of the English climate, the glory of the whole day went out with the sunshine. The woods suddenly became wrinkled and gray, the distant hills sombre, the very English turf beneath her feet grew brown; a mile and a half away, through the opening of the trees, the west part of the Priory looked a crumbling, ivy-eaten ruin. A few drops of rain fell. She hurried on. Suddenly she remembered that the avenue made a long circuit before approaching the house, and that its lower end, where she was walking, was but a fringe of the park. Consequently there must be a short cut across some fields and farm buildings to the back of the park and the Priory. She at once diverged to the right, presently found a low fence, which she clambered over, and again found a footpath which led to a stile. Crossing that, she could see the footpath now led directly to the Priory,—now a grim and austere looking pile in the suddenly dejected landscape,— and that it was probably used only by the servants and farmers. A gust of wind brought some swift needles of rain to her cheek; she could see the sad hills beyond the Priory already veiling their faces; she gathered her skirts and ran. The next field was a long one, but beside the further stile was a small clump of trees, the only ones between her and the park. Hurrying on to that shelter, she saw that the stile was already occupied by a tall but bent figure, holding a long stick in his hand, which gave him the appearance, against the horizon, of the figure of Time leaning on his scythe. As she came nearer she saw it was, indeed, an old man, half resting on his rake. He was very rugged and weather-beaten, and although near the shelter of the trees, apparently unmindful of the rain that was falling on his bald head, and the limp cap he was holding uselessly in one hand. He was staring at her, yet apparently unconscious of her presence. A sudden instinct came upon her—it was "Debs"!

She went directly up to him, and with that frank common sense which ordinarily distinguished her, took his cap from his hand and put it on his head, grasped his arm firmly, and led him to the shelter of the tree. Then she wiped the raindrops from his face with her handkerchief, shook out her own dress and her wet parasol, and, propping her companion against the tree, said:—

"There, Mr. Debs! I've heard of people who didn't know enough to come in when it rained, but I never met one before."

The old man started, lifted his hairy, sinewy arm, bared to the elbow, and wiped his bare throat with the dry side of it. Then a look of intelligence—albeit half aggressive—came into his face. "Wheer beest tha going?" he asked.

Something in his voice struck Sadie like a vague echo. Perhaps it was only the queer dialect—or some resemblance to his granddaughter's voice. She looked at him a little more closely as she said:—

"To the Priory."

"Whaat?"

She pointed with her parasol to the gray pile in the distance. It was possible that this demented peasant didn't even UNDERSTAND English.

"The hall. Oh, ay!" Suddenly his brows knit ominously as he faced her. "An' wassist tha doin' drest oop in this foinery? Wheer gettist thee that goawn? Thissen, or thy maester? Nowt even a napron, fit for thy wark as maaid at serviss; an' parson a gettin' tha plaace at Hall! So thou'lt be high and moity will tha! thou'lt not walk wi' maaids, but traipse by thissen like a slut in the toon—dang tha!"

Although it was plain to Sadie that the old man, in his wandering perception, had mistaken her for his grand-daughter in service at the Priory, there was still enough rudeness in his speech for her to have resented it. But, strange to say, there was a kind of authority in it that touched her with an uneasiness and repulsion that was stronger than any other feeling. "I think you have mistaken me for some one else," she said hurriedly, yet wondering why she had admitted it, and even irritated at the admission. "I am a stranger here, a visitor at the Priory. I called with Miss Amelyn at your cottage, and saw your other granddaughter; that's how I knew your name."

The old man's face changed. A sad, senile smile of hopeless bewilderment crept into his hard mouth; he plucked his limp cap from his head and let it hang submissively in his fingers, as if it were his sole apology. Then he tried to straighten himself, and said, "Naw offins, miss, naw offins! If tha knaws mea tha'll knaw I'm grandfeyther to two galls as moight be tha owern age; tha'll tell 'ee that old Debs at haaty years 'as warked and niver lost a day as man or boy; has niver coome oopen 'em for n'aporth. An' 'e'll keep out o' warkus till he doy. An' 'ee's put by enow to by wi' his own feythers in Lanksheer, an' not liggen aloane in parson's choorchyard."

It was part of her uneasiness that, scarcely understanding or, indeed, feeling any interest in these maundering details, she still seemed to have an odd comprehension of his character and some reminiscent knowledge of him, as if she were going through the repetition of some unpleasant dream. Even his wrinkled face was becoming familiar to her. Some weird attraction was holding her; she wanted to get away from it as much as she wanted to analyze it. She glanced ostentatiously at the sky, prepared to open her parasol, and began to edge cautiously away.

"Then tha beant from these pearts?" he said suddenly.

"No, no," she said quickly and emphatically,—"no, I'm an American."

The old man started and moved towards her, eagerly, his keen eyes breaking through the film that at times obscured them. "'Merrikan! tha baist 'Merrikan? Then tha knaws ma son John, 'ee war nowt but a bairn when brether Dick took un to 'Merriky! Naw! Now! that wor fifty years sen!—niver wroate to his old feyther—niver coomed back, 'Ee wor tall-loike, an' thea said 'e feavored mea." He stopped, threw up his head, and with his skinny fingers drew back his long, straggling locks from his sunken cheeks, and stared in her face. The quick transition of fascination, repulsion, shock, and indefinable apprehension made her laugh hysterically. To her terror he joined in it, and eagerly clasped her wrists. "Eh, lass! tha knaws John—tha coomes from un to ole grandfeyther. Who-rr-u! Eay! but tha tho't to fool mea, did tha, lass? Whoy, I knoawed tha voice, for a' tha foine peacock feathers. So tha be John's gell coom from Ameriky.

Dear! a dear! Coom neaur, lass! let's see what tha's loike. Eh, but thou'lt kiss tha grandfather, sewerly?"

A wild terror and undefined consternation had completely overpowered her! But she made a desperate effort to free her wrists, and burst out madly:—

"Let me go! How dare you! I don't know you or yours! I'm nothing to you or your kin! My name is Desborough—do you understand—do you hear me, Mr. Debs?— DESBOROUGH!"

At the word the old man's fingers stiffened like steel around her wrists, as he turned upon her a hard, invincible face.

"So thou'lt call thissen Des-borough, wilt tha? Let me tell tha, then, that 'Debs,' 'Debban,' 'Debbrook,' and 'Des-borough' are all a seame! Ay! thy feyther and thy feyther's feyther! Thou'lt be a Des-borough, will tha? Dang tha! and look doon on tha kin, and dress thissen in silks o' shame! Tell 'ee thou'rt an ass, gell! Don't tha hear? An ass! for all tha bean John's bairn! An ass! that's what tha beast!"

With flashing eyes and burning cheeks she made one more supreme effort, lifting her arms, freeing her wrists, and throwing the old man staggering from her. Then she leaped the stile, turned, and fled through the rain. But before she reached the end of the field she stopped! She had freed herself—she was stronger than he—what had she to fear? He was crazy! Yes, he MUST be crazy, and he had insulted her, but he was an old man—and God knows what! Her heart was beating rapidly, her breath was hurried, but she ran back to the stile.

He was not there. The field sloped away on either side of it. But she could distinguish nothing in the pouring rain above the wind-swept meadow. He must have gone home. Relieved for a moment she turned and hurried on towards the Priory.

But at every step she was followed, not by the old man's presence, but by what he had said to her, which she could not shake off as she had shaken off his detaining fingers. Was it the ravings of insanity, or had she stumbled unwittingly upon some secret—was it after all a SECRET? Perhaps it was something they all knew, or would know later. And she had come down here for this. For back of her indignation, back even of her disbelief in his insanity, there was an awful sense of truth! The names he had flung out, of "Debs," "Debban," and "Debbrook" now flashed upon her as something she had seen before, but had not understood. Until she satisfied herself of this, she felt she could not live or breathe! She loathed the Priory, with its austere exclusiveness, as it rose before her; she wished she had never entered it; but it contained that which she must know, and know at once! She entered the nearest door and ran up the grand staircase. Her flushed face and disordered appearance were easily accounted for by her exposure to the sudden storm. She went to her bedroom, sent her maid to another room to prepare a change of dress, and sinking down before her traveling-desk, groped for a document. Ah! there it was—the expensive toy that she had played with! She hastily ran over its leaves to the page she already remembered. And there, among the dashes and perpendicular lines she had jested over last night, on which she had thought was a collateral branch of the line, stood her father's name and that of Richard, his uncle, with the bracketed note in red ink, "see Debbrook, Daybrook, Debbers, and Debs." Yes! this gaunt, half-crazy, overworked peasant, content to rake the dead leaves before the rolling chariots of the Beverdales, was her grandfather; that poorly clad girl in the cottage, and even the menial in the scullery of this very house that might be HERS, were her COUSINS! She burst into a laugh, and then refolded the document and put it away.

At luncheon she was radiant and sparkling. Her drenched clothes were an excuse for a new and ravishing toilette. She had never looked so beautiful before, and significant glances were exchanged between some of the guests, who believed that the expected proposal had already come. But those who were of the carriage party knew otherwise, and of Lord Algernon's disappointment. Lord Beverdale contented himself with rallying his fair guest on the becomingness of "good works." But he continued, "You're offering a dreadful example to these ladies, Miss Desborough, and I know I shall never hereafter be able to content them with any frivolous morning amusement at the Priory. For myself, when I am grown gouty and hideous, I know I shall bloom again as a district visitor."

Yet under this surface sparkle and nervous exaltation Sadie never lost consciousness of the gravity of the situation. If her sense of humor enabled her to see one side of its grim irony; if she experienced a wicked satisfaction in accepting the admiration and easy confidence of the high-born guests, knowing that her cousin had assisted in preparing the meal they were eating, she had never lost sight of the practical effect of the discovery she had made. And she had come to a final resolution. She should leave the Priory at once, and abandon all idea of a matrimonial alliance with its heir! Inconsistent as this might seem to her selfish, worldly nature, it was nevertheless in keeping with a certain pride and independence that was in her blood. She did not love Lord Algernon, neither did she love her grandfather; she was equally willing to sacrifice either or both; she knew that neither Lord Algernon nor his father would make her connections an objection, however they might wish to keep the fact a secret, or otherwise dispose of them by pensions or emigration, but she could not bear to KNOW IT HERSELF!

She never could be happy as the mistress of Scrooby Priory with that knowledge; she did not idealize it as a principle! Carefully weighing it by her own practical common sense, she said to herself that "it wouldn't pay." The highest independence is often akin to the lowest selfishness; she did not dream that the same pride which kept her grandfather from the workhouse and support by his daughters, and had even kept him from communicating with his own son, now kept her from acknowledging them, even for the gift of a title and domain. There was only one question before her: should she stay long enough to receive the proposal of Lord Algernon, and then decline it? Why should she not snatch that single feminine joy out of the ashes of her burnt-up illusion? She knew that an opportunity would be offered that afternoon. The party were to take tea at Broxby Hall, and Lord Algernon was to drive her there in his dogcart. Miss Desborough had gone up to her bedroom to put on a warmer cloak, and had rung twice or thrice impatiently for her maid.

When the girl made her appearance, apologetic, voluble, and excited, Miss Desborough scarcely listened to her excuses, until a single word suddenly arrested her attention. It was "old Debs."

"What ARE you talking about?" said Sadie, pausing in the adjustment of her hat on her brown hair.

"Old Debs, miss,—that's what they call him; an old park-keeper, just found dead in a pool of water in the fields; the grandfather of one of the servants here; and there's such an excitement in the servants' hall. The gentlemen all knew it, too, for I heard Lord Algernon say that he was looking very queer lately, and might have had a fit; and Lord Beverdale has sent word to the coroner. And only think, the people here are such fools that they daren't touch or move the poor man, and him lyin' there in the rain all the time, until the coroner comes!"

Miss Desborough had been steadily regarding herself in the glass to see if she had turned pale. She had. She set her teeth together until the color partly returned. But she kept her face away from the maid. "That'll do," she said quietly. "You can tell me all later. I have some important news myself, and I may not go out after all. I want you to take a note for me." She went to her table, wrote a line in pencil, folded it, scribbled an address upon it, handed it to the girl, and gently pushed her from the room.

*****

The consul was lingering on the terrace beside one of the carriages; at a little distance a groom was holding the nervous thoroughbred of Lord Algernon's dog-cart. Suddenly he felt a touch on his shoulder, and Miss Desborough's maid put a note in his hand. It contained only a line:—

Please come and see me in the library, but without making any fuss about it—at once. S. D.

The consul glanced around him; no one had apparently noticed the incident. He slipped back into the house and made his way to the library. It was a long gallery; at the further end Miss Desborough stood cloaked, veiled, and coquettishly hatted. She was looking very beautiful and animated. "I want you to please do me a great favor," she said, with an adorable smile, "as your own countrywoman, you know—for the sake of Fourth of July and Pumpkin Pie and the Old Flag! I don't want to go to this circus to-day. I am going to leave here to-night! I am! Honest Injin! I want YOU to manage it. I want you to say that as consul you've received important news for me: the death of some relative, if you like; or better, something AFFECTING MY PROPERTY, you know," with a little satirical laugh. "I guess that would fetch 'em! So go at once."

"But really, Miss Desborough, do let us talk this over before you decide!" implored the bewildered consul. "Think what a disappointment to your host and these ladies. Lord Algernon expects to drive you there; he is already waiting! The party was got up for you!" Miss Desborough made a slight grimace. "I mean you ought to sacrifice something—but I trust there is really nothing serious—to them!"

"If YOU do not speak to them, I will!" said Miss Desborough firmly. "If you say what I tell you, it will come the more plausibly from you. Come! My mind is made up. One of us must break the news! Shall it be you or I?" She drew her cloak over her shoulders and made a step forwards.

The consul saw she was determined. "Then wait here till I return, but keep yourself out of sight," he said, and hurried away. Between the library and the terrace he conceived a plan. His perplexity lent him a seriousness which befitted the gravity of the news he had to disclose. "I am sorry to have to tell you," he said, taking Lord Beverdale aside, "that I was the unlucky bearer of some sad news to Miss Desborough this morning, through my consular letters—some matter concerning the death of a relation of hers, and some wearisome question of property. I thought that it was of little importance, and that she would not take it seriously, but I find I was mistaken. It may even oblige her to catch the London train to-night. I promised to make her excuses to you for the present, and I'm afraid I must add my own to them, as she wishes me to stay and advise her in this matter, which requires some prompt action."

Miss Desborough was right: the magic word "property"

changed the slight annoyance on the earl's face to a sympathetic concern. "Dear me! I trust it is nothing really serious," he said. "Of course, you will advise her, and, by the way, if my solicitor, Withers, who'll be here to-morrow, can do anything, you know, call him in. I hope she'll be able to see me later. It could not be a NEAR relation who died, I fancy; she has no brothers or sisters, I understand."

"A cousin, I think; an old friend," said the consul hastily. He heard Lord Beverdale say a few words to his companions, saw with a tinge of remorse a cloud settle upon Lord Algernon's fresh face, as he appealed in a whisper to old Lady Mesthyn, who leaned forward from the carriage, and said, "If the dear child thought I could be of any service, I should only be too glad to stay with her."

"I knew she would appreciate Lady Mesthyn's sympathy," said the ingenious consul quickly, "but I really think the question is more a business one—and"—

"Ah, yes," said the old lady, shaking her head, "it's dreadful, of course, but we must all think of THAT!"

As the carriage drove away, the consul hurried back a little viciously to his fair countrywoman. "There!" he said, "I have done it! If I have managed to convey either the idea that you are a penniless orphan, or that I have official information that you are suspected of a dynamite conspiracy, don't blame me! And now," he said, "as I have excused myself on the ground that I must devote myself to this dreadful business of yours, perhaps you'll tell me WHAT it really is."

"Not a word more," said Miss Desborough; "except," she added,—checking her smile with a weary gesture,—"except that I want to leave this dreadful place at once! There! don't ask me any more!"

There could be no doubt of the girl's sincerity. Nor was it the extravagant caprice of a petted idol. What had happened? He might have believed in a lovers' quarrel, but he knew that she and Lord Algernon could have had no private interview that evening. He must perforce accept her silence, yet he could not help saying:—

"You seemed to like the place so much last night. I say, you haven't seen the Priory ghost, have you?"

"The Priory ghost," she said quickly. "What's that?"

"The old monk who passes through the cloisters with the sacred oil, the bell, and the smell of incense whenever any one is to die here. By Jove! it would have been a good story to tell instead of this cock-and-bull one about your property. And there WAS a death here to-day. You'd have added the sibyl's gifts to your other charms."

"Tell me about that old man," she said, looking past him out of the window. "I was at his cottage this morning. But, no! first let us go out. You can take me for a walk, if you like. You see I am all ready, and I'm just stifling here."

They descended to the terrace together. "Where would you like to go?" he asked.

"To the village. I may want to telegraph, you know."

They turned into the avenue, but Miss Desborough stopped.

"Is there not a shorter cut across the fields," she asked, "over there?"

"There is," said the consul.

They both turned into the footpath which led to the farm and stile. After a pause she said, "Did you ever talk with that poor old man?"

"No."

"Then you don't know if he really was crazy, as they think."

"No. But they may have thought an old man's forgetfulness of present things and his habit of communing with the past was insanity. For all that he was a plucky, independent old fellow, with a grim purpose that was certainly rational."

"I suppose in his independence he would not have taken favors from these people, or anybody?"

"I should think not."

"Don't you think it was just horrid—their leaving him alone in the rain, when he might have been only in a fit?"

"The doctor says he died suddenly of heart disease," said the consul. "It might have happened at any moment and without warning."

"Ah, that was the coroner's verdict, then," said Miss Desborough quickly.

"The coroner did not think it necessary to have any inquest after Lord Beverdale's statement. It wouldn't have been very joyous for the Priory party. And I dare say he thought it might not be very cheerful for YOU."

"How very kind!" said the young girl, with a quick laugh. "But do you know that it's about the only thing human, original, and striking that has happened in this place since

I've been here! And so unexpected, considering how comfortably everything is ordered here beforehand."

"Yet you seemed to like that kind of thing very well, last evening," said the consul mischievously.

"That was last night," retorted Miss Desborough; "and you know the line, 'Colors seen by candlelight do not look the same by day.' But I'm going to be very consistent to-day, for I intend to go over to that poor man's cottage again, and see if I can be of any service. Will you go with me?"

"Certainly," said the consul, mystified by his companion's extraordinary conduct, yet apparent coolness of purpose, and hoping for some further explanation. Was she only an inexperienced flirt who had found herself on the point of a serious entanglement she had not contemplated? Yet even then he knew she was clever enough to extricate herself in some other way than this abrupt and brutal tearing through the meshes. Or was it possible that she really had any intelligence affecting her property? He reflected that he knew very little of the Desboroughs, but on the other hand he knew that Beverdale knew them much better, and was a prudent man. He had no right to demand her confidence as a reward for his secrecy; he must wait her pleasure. Perhaps she would still explain; women seldom could resist the triumph of telling the secret that puzzled others.

When they reached the village she halted before the low roof of Debs's cottage. "I had better go in first," she said; "you can come in later, and in the meantime you might go to the station for me and find out the exact time that the express train leaves for the north."

"But," said the astonished consul, "I thought you were going to London?"

"No," said Miss Desborough quietly, "I am going to join some friends at Harrogate."

"But that train goes much earlier than the train south, and— and I'm afraid Lord Beverdale will not have returned so soon."

"How sad!" said Miss Desborough, with a faint smile, "but we must bear up under it, and—I'll write him. I will be here until you return."

She turned away and entered the cottage. The granddaughter she had already seen and her sister, the servant at the Priory, were both chatting comfortably, but ceased as she entered, and both rose with awkward respect. There was little to suggest that the body of their grandfather, already in a rough oak shell, was lying upon trestles beside them.

"You have carried out my orders, I see," said Miss Desborough, laying down her parasol.

"Ay, miss; but it was main haard gettin' et dooan so soon, and et cooast"—

"Never mind the cost. I've given you money enough, I think, and if I haven't, I guess I can give you more."

"Ay, miss! Abbut the pa'son 'ead gi' un a funeral for nowt."

"But I understood you to say," said Miss Desborough, with an impatient flash of eye, "that your grandfather wished to be buried with his kindred in the north?"

"Ay, miss," said the girl apologetically, "an naw 'ees savit th' munny. Abbut e'd bean tickled 'ad 'ee knowed it! Dear! dear! 'ee niver thowt et 'ud be gi'en by stranger an' not 'es ownt fammaly."

"For all that, you needn't tell anybody it was given by ME," said Miss Desborough. "And you'll be sure to be ready to take the train this afternoon—without delay." There was a certain peremptoriness in her voice very unlike Miss Amelyn's, yet apparently much more effective with the granddaughter.

"Ay, miss. Then, if tha'll excoose mea, I'll go streight to 'oory oop sexten."

She bustled away. "Now," said Miss Desborough, turning to the other girl, "I shall take the same train, and will probably see you on the platform at York to give my final directions. That's all. Go and see if the gentleman who came with me has returned from the station."

The girl obeyed. Left entirely alone, Miss Desborough glanced around the room, and then went quietly up to the unlidded coffin. The repose of death had softened the hard lines of the old man's mouth and brow into a resemblance she now more than ever understood. She had stood thus only a few years before, looking at the same face in a gorgeously inlaid mahogany casket, smothered amidst costly flowers, and surrounded by friends attired in all the luxurious trappings of woe; yet it was the same face that was now rigidly upturned to the bare thatch and rafters of that crumbling cottage, herself its only companion. She lifted her delicate veil with both hands, and, stooping down, kissed the hard, cold forehead, without a tremor. Then she dropped her veil again over her dry eyes, readjusted it in the little, cheap, black-framed mirror that hung against the wall, and opened the door as the granddaughter returned. The gentleman was just coming from the station.

"Remember to look out for me at York," said Miss Desborough, extending her gloved hand. "Good-by till then." The young girl respectfully touched the ends of Miss Desborough's fingers, dropped a curtsy, and Miss Desborough rejoined the consul.

"You have barely time to return to the Priory and see to your luggage," said the consul, "if you must go. But let me hope that you have changed your mind."

"I have not changed my mind," said Miss Desborough quietly, "and my baggage is already packed." After a pause, she said thoughtfully, "I've been wondering"—

"What?" said the consul eagerly.

"I've been wondering if people brought up to speak in a certain dialect, where certain words have their own significance and color, and are part of their own lives and experience—if, even when they understand another dialect, they really feel any sympathy with it, or the person who speaks it?"

"Apropos of"—asked the consul.

"These people I've just left! I don't think I quite felt with them, and I guess they didn't feel with me."

"But," said the consul laughingly, "you know that we Americans speak with a decided dialect of our own, and attach the same occult meaning to it. Yet, upon my word, I think that Lord Beverdale—or shall I say Lord Algernon?— would not only understand that American word 'guess' as you mean it, but would perfectly sympathize with you."

Miss Desborough's eyes sparkled even through her veil as

she glanced at her companion and said, "I GUESS NOT."

As the "tea" party had not yet returned, it fell to the consul to accompany Miss Desborough and her maid to the station. But here he was startled to find a collection of villagers upon the platform, gathered round two young women in mourning, and an ominous-looking box. He mingled for a moment with the crowd, and then returned to Miss Desborough's side.

"Really," he said, with a concern that was scarcely assumed, "I ought not to let you go. The omens are most disastrous! You came here to a death; you are going away with a funeral!"

"Then it's high time I took myself off!" said the lady lightly.

"Unless, like the ghostly monk, you came here on a mission, and have fulfilled it."

"Perhaps I have. Good-by!"

*****

In spite of the bright and characteristic letter which Miss Desborough left for her host,—a letter which mingled her peculiar shrewd sense with her humorous extravagance of expression,—the consul spent a somewhat uneasy evening under the fire of questions that assailed him in reference to the fair deserter. But he kept loyal faith with her, adhering even to the letter of her instructions, and only once was goaded into more active mendacity. The conversation had turned upon "Debs," and the consul had remarked on the singularity of the name. A guest from the north observed, however, that the name was undoubtedly a contraction. "Possibly it might have been 'Debborough,' or even the same name as our fair friend."

"But didn't Miss Desborough tell you last night that she had been hunting up her people, with a family tree, or something like that?" said Lord Algernon eagerly. "I just caught a word here and there, for you were both laughing."

The consul smiled blandly. "You may well say so, for it was all the most delightful piece of pure invention and utter extravagance. It would have amused her still more if she had thought you were listening and took it seriously!"

"Of course; I see!" said the young fellow, with a laugh and a slight rise of color. "I knew she was taking some kind of a rise out of YOU, and that remark reminded me of it."

Nevertheless, within a year, Lord Algernon was happily married to the daughter of a South African millionaire, whose bridal offerings alone touched the sum of half a million. It was also said that the mother was "impossible" and the father "unspeakable," the relations "inextinguishable;" but the wedding was an "occasion," and in the succeeding year of festivity it is presumed that the names of "Debs" and "Desborough" were alike forgotten.

But they existed still in a little hamlet near the edge of a bleak northern moor, where they were singularly exalted on a soaring shaft of pure marble above the submerged and moss-grown tombstones of a simple country churchyard. So great was the contrast between the modern and pretentious monument and the graves of the humbler forefathers of the village, that even the Americans who chanced to visit it were shocked at what they believed was the ostentatious and vulgar pride of one of their own countrywomen. For on its pedestal was inscribed:—

Sacred to the Memory
Of

JOHN DEBS DESBOROUGH,
Formerly of this parish,
Who departed this life October 20th, 1892,
At Scrooby Priory,
At the age of eighty-two years.
This monument was erected as a loving testimony
by his granddaughter,
Sadie Desborough, of New York, U. S. A.

"And evening brings us home."

SALOMY JANE'S KISS

Only one shot had been fired. It had gone wide of its mark,—the ringleader of the Vigilantes,—and had left Red Pete, who had fired it, covered by their rifles and at their mercy. For his hand had been cramped by hard riding, and his eye distracted by their sudden onset, and so the inevitable end had come. He submitted sullenly to his captors; his companion fugitive and horse-thief gave up the protracted struggle with a feeling not unlike relief. Even the hot and revengeful victors were content. They had taken their men alive. At any time during the long chase they could have brought them down by a rifle shot, but it would have been unsportsmanlike, and have ended in a free fight, instead of an example. And, for the matter of that, their doom was already sealed. Their end, by a rope and a tree, although not sanctified by law, would have at least the deliberation of justice. It was the tribute paid by the Vigilantes to that order which they had themselves disregarded in the pursuit and capture. Yet this strange logic of the frontier sufficed them, and gave a certain dignity to the climax.

"Ef you've got anything to say to your folks, say it NOW, and say it quick," said the ringleader.

Red Pete glanced around him. He had been run to earth at his own cabin in the clearing, whence a few relations and friends, mostly women and children, non-combatants, had outflowed, gazing vacantly at the twenty Vigilantes who surrounded them. All were accustomed to scenes of violence, blood-feud, chase, and hardship; it was only the suddenness of the onset and its quick result that had surprised them. They looked on with dazed curiosity and some disappointment; there had been no fight to speak of—no spectacle! A boy, nephew of Red Pete, got upon the rain-barrel to view the proceedings more comfortably; a tall, handsome, lazy Kentucky girl, a visiting neighbor, leaned against the doorpost, chewing gum. Only a yellow hound was actively perplexed. He could not make out if a hunt were just over or beginning, and ran eagerly backwards and forwards, leaping alternately upon the captives and the captors.

The ringleader repeated his challenge. Red Pete gave a reckless laugh and looked at his wife.

At which Mrs. Red Pete came forward. It seemed that she had much to say, incoherently, furiously, vindictively, to the ringleader. His soul would roast in hell for that day's work! He called himself a man, skunkin' in the open and afraid to show himself except with a crowd of other "Kiyi's" around a house of women and children. Heaping insult upon insult, inveighing against his low blood, his ancestors, his dubious origin, she at last flung out a wild taunt of his invalid wife, the insult of a woman to a woman, until his white face grew rigid, and only that Western-American fetich of the sanctity of sex kept his twitching fingers from the lock of his rifle. Even her husband noticed it, and with a half-authoritative "Let up on that, old gal," and a pat of his freed left hand on her back, took his last parting. The ringleader, still white under the lash of the woman's tongue, turned abruptly to the second captive. "And if YOU'VE got anybody to say 'good-by' to, now's your chance."

The man looked up. Nobody stirred or spoke. He was a stranger there, being a chance confederate picked up by Red Pete, and known to no one. Still young, but an outlaw from his abandoned boyhood, of which father and mother were only a forgotten dream, he loved horses and stole them, fully accepting the frontier penalty of life for the interference with that animal on which a man's life so often depended. But he understood the good points of a horse, as was shown by the ones he bestrode—until a few days before the property of Judge Boompointer. This was his sole distinction.

The unexpected question stirred him for a moment out of the attitude of reckless indifference, for attitude it was, and a part of his profession. But it may have touched him that at that moment he was less than his companion and his virago wife. However, he only shook his head. As he did so his eye casually fell on the handsome girl by the doorpost, who was looking at him. The ringleader, too, may have been touched by his complete loneliness, for HE hesitated. At the same moment he saw that the girl was looking at his friendless captive.

A grotesque idea struck him.

"Salomy Jane, ye might do worse than come yere and say 'good-by' to a dying man, and him a stranger," he said.

There seemed to be a subtle stroke of poetry and irony in this that equally struck the apathetic crowd. It was well known that Salomy Jane Clay thought no small potatoes of herself, and always held off the local swain with a lazy nymph-like scorn. Nevertheless, she slowly disengaged herself from the doorpost, and, to everybody's astonishment, lounged with languid grace and outstretched hand towards the prisoner. The color came into the gray reckless mask which the doomed man wore as her right hand grasped his left, just loosed by his captors. Then she paused; her shy, fawn-like eyes grew bold, and fixed themselves upon him. She took the chewing-gum from her mouth, wiped her red lips with the back of her hand, by a sudden lithe spring placed her foot on his stirrup, and, bounding to the saddle, threw her arms about his neck and pressed a kiss upon his lips.

They remained thus for a hushed moment—the man on the threshold of death, the young woman in the fullness of youth and beauty—linked together. Then the crowd laughed; in the audacious effrontery of the girl's act the ultimate fate of the two men was forgotten. She slipped languidly to the ground; SHE was the focus of all eyes,—she only! The ringleader saw it and his opportunity. He shouted: "Time's up— Forward!" urged his horse beside his captives, and the next moment the whole cavalcade was sweeping over the clearing into the darkening woods.

Their destination was Sawyer's Crossing, the headquarters of the committee, where the council was still sitting, and where both culprits were to expiate the offense of which that council had already found them guilty. They rode in great and breathless haste,—a haste in which, strangely enough, even the captives seemed to join. That haste possibly prevented them from noticing the singular change which had taken place in the second captive since the episode of the kiss. His high color remained, as if it had burned through his mask of indifference; his eyes were quick, alert, and keen, his mouth half open as if the girl's kiss still lingered there. And that haste had made them careless, for the horse of the man who led him slipped in a gopher-hole, rolled over, unseated his rider, and even dragged the bound and helpless second captive from Judge Boompointer's favorite mare. In an instant they were all on their feet again, but in that supreme moment the second captive felt the cords which bound his arms had slipped to his wrists. By keeping his elbows to his sides, and obliging the others to help him mount, it escaped their notice. By riding close to his captors, and keeping in the crush of the throng, he further concealed the accident, slowly working his hands downwards out of his bonds.

Their way lay through a sylvan wilderness, mid-leg deep in ferns, whose tall fronds brushed their horses' sides in their furious gallop and concealed the flapping of the captive's loosened cords. The peaceful vista, more suggestive of the offerings of nymph and shepherd than of human sacrifice, was in a strange contrast to this whirlwind rush of stern, armed men. The westering sun pierced the subdued light and the tremor of leaves with yellow lances; birds started into song on blue and dove-like wings, and on either side of the trail of this vengeful storm could be heard the murmur of hidden and tranquil waters. In a few moments they would be on the open ridge, whence sloped the common turnpike to "Sawyer's," a mile away. It was the custom of returning cavalcades to take this hill at headlong speed, with shouts and cries that heralded their coming. They withheld the latter that day, as inconsistent with their dignity; but, emerging from the wood, swept silently like an avalanche down the slope. They were well under way, looking only to their horses, when the second captive slipped his right arm from the bonds and succeeded in grasping the reins that lay trailing on the horse's neck. A sudden vaquero jerk, which the well-trained animal understood, threw him on his haunches with his forelegs firmly planted on the slope. The rest of the cavalcade swept on; the man who was leading the captive's horse by the riata, thinking only of another accident, dropped the line to save himself from being dragged backwards from his horse. The captive wheeled, and the next moment was galloping furiously up the slope.

It was the work of a moment; a trained horse and an

experienced hand. The cavalcade had covered nearly fifty yards before they could pull up; the freed captive had covered half that distance uphill. The road was so narrow that only two shots could be fired, and these broke dust two yards ahead of the fugitive. They had not dared to fire low; the horse was the more valuable animal. The fugitive knew this in his extremity also, and would have gladly taken a shot in his own leg to spare that of his horse. Five men were detached to recapture or kill him. The latter seemed inevitable. But he had calculated his chances; before they could reload he had reached the woods again; winding in and out between the pillared tree trunks, he offered no mark. They knew his horse was superior to their own; at the end of two hours they returned, for he had disappeared without track or trail. The end was briefly told in the "Sierra Record:"—

"Red Pete, the notorious horse-thief, who had so long eluded justice, was captured and hung by the Sawyer's Crossing Vigilantes last week; his confederate, unfortunately, escaped on a valuable horse belonging to Judge Boompointer. The judge had refused one thousand dollars for the horse only a week before. As the thief, who is still at large, would find it difficult to dispose of so valuable an animal without detection, the chances are against either of them turning up again."

*****

Salomy Jane watched the cavalcade until it had disappeared. Then she became aware that her brief popularity had passed. Mrs. Red Pete, in stormy hysterics, had included her in a sweeping denunciation of the whole universe, possibly for simulating an emotion in which she herself was deficient. The other women hated her for her momentary exaltation above them; only the children still admired her as one who had undoubtedly "canoodled" with a man "a-going to be hung"—a daring flight beyond their wildest ambition. Salomy Jane accepted the change with charming unconcern. She put on her yellow nankeen sunbonnet,—a hideous affair that would have ruined any other woman, but which only enhanced the piquancy of her fresh brunette skin,—tied the strings, letting the blue-black braids escape below its frilled curtain behind, jumped on her mustang with a casual display of agile ankles in shapely white stockings, whistled to the hound, and waving her hand with a "So long, sonny!" to the lately bereft but admiring nephew, flapped and fluttered away in her short brown holland gown.

Her father's house was four miles distant. Contrasted with the cabin she had just quitted, it was a superior dwelling, with a long "lean-to" at the rear, which brought the eaves almost to the ground and made it look like a low triangle. It had a long barn and cattle sheds, for Madison Clay was a "great" stock-raiser and the owner of a "quarter section." It had a sitting-room and a parlor organ, whose transportation thither had been a marvel of "packing." These things were supposed to give Salomy Jane an undue importance, but the girl's reserve and inaccessibility to local advances were rather the result of a cool, lazy temperament and the preoccupation of a large, protecting admiration for her father, for some years a widower. For Mr. Madison Clay's life had been threatened in one or two feuds,—it was said, not without cause,—and it is possible that the pathetic spectacle of her father doing his visiting with a shotgun may have touched her closely and somewhat prejudiced her against the neighboring masculinity. The thought that cattle, horses, and "quarter section" would one day be hers did not disturb her calm. As for Mr. Clay, he accepted her as housewifely, though somewhat "interfering," and, being one of "his own womankind," therefore not without some degree of merit.

"Wot's this yer I'm hearin' of your doin's over at Red Pete's? Honeyfoglin' with a horse-thief, eh?" said Mr. Clay two days later at breakfast.

"I reckon you heard about the straight thing, then," said Salomy Jane unconcernedly, without looking round.

"What do you kalkilate Rube will say to it? What are you goin' to tell HIM?" said Mr. Clay sarcastically.

"Rube," or Reuben Waters, was a swain supposed to be favored particularly by Mr. Clay. Salomy Jane looked up.

"I'll tell him that when HE'S on his way to be hung, I'll kiss him,—not till then," said the young lady brightly.

This delightful witticism suited the paternal humor, and Mr. Clay smiled; but, nevertheless, he frowned a moment afterwards.

"But this yer hoss-thief got away arter all, and that's a hoss of a different color," he said grimly.

Salomy Jane put down her knife and fork. This was certainly a new and different phase of the situation. She had never thought of it before, and, strangely enough, for the first time she became interested in the man. "Got away?" she repeated. "Did they let him off?"

"Not much," said her father briefly. "Slipped his cords, and going down the grade pulled up short, just like a vaquero agin a lassoed bull, almost draggin' the man leadin' him off his hoss, and then skyuted up the grade. For that matter, on that hoss o' Judge Boompointer's he mout have dragged the whole posse of 'em down on their knees ef he liked! Sarved 'em right, too. Instead of stringin' him up afore the door, or shootin' him on sight, they must allow to take him down afore the hull committee 'for an example.' 'Example' be blowed! Ther' 's example enough when some stranger comes unbeknownst slap onter a man hanged to a tree and plugged full of holes. THAT'S an example, and HE knows what it means. Wot more do ye want? But then those Vigilantes is allus clingin' and hangin' onter some mere scrap o' the law they're pretendin' to despise. It makes me sick! Why, when Jake Myers shot your ole Aunt Viney's second husband, and I laid in wait for Jake afterwards in the Butternut Hollow, did I tie him to his hoss and fetch him down to your Aunt Viney's cabin 'for an example' before I plugged him? No!" in deep disgust. "No! Why, I just meandered through the wood, careless-like, till he comes out, and I just rode up to him, and I said"—

But Salomy Jane had heard her father's story before. Even one's dearest relatives are apt to become tiresome in narration. "I know, dad," she interrupted; "but this yer man,—this hoss-thief,—did HE get clean away without gettin' hurt at all?"

"He did, and unless he's fool enough to sell the hoss he kin keep away, too. So ye see, ye can't ladle out purp stuff about a 'dyin' stranger' to Rube. He won't swaller it."

"All the same, dad," returned the girl cheerfully, "I reckon to say it, and say MORE; I'll tell him that ef HE manages to get away too, I'll marry him—there! But ye don't ketch Rube takin' any such risks in gettin' ketched, or in gettin' away arter!"

Madison Clay smiled grimly, pushed back his chair, rose, dropped a perfunctory kiss on his daughter's hair, and, taking his shotgun from the corner, departed on a peaceful Samaritan mission to a cow who had dropped a calf in the far pasture. Inclined as he was to Reuben's wooing from his eligibility as to property, he was conscious that he was sadly deficient in certain qualities inherent in the Clay family. It certainly would be a kind of mesalliance.

Left to herself, Salomy Jane stared a long while at the coffee-pot, and then called the two squaws who assisted her in her household duties, to clear away the things while she went up to her own room to make her bed. Here she was confronted with a possible prospect of that proverbial bed she might be making in her willfulness, and on which she must lie, in the photograph of a somewhat serious young man of refined features—Reuben Waters—stuck in her window-frame. Salomy Jane smiled over her last witticism regarding him and enjoyed, it, like your true humorist, and then, catching sight of her own handsome face in the little mirror, smiled again. But wasn't it funny about that horse-thief getting off after all? Good Lordy! Fancy Reuben hearing he was alive and going round with that kiss of hers set on his lips! She laughed again, a little more abstractedly. And he had returned it like a man, holding her tight and almost breathless, and he going to be hung the next minute! Salomy Jane had been kissed at other times, by force, chance, or stratagem. In a certain ingenuous forfeit game of the locality known as "I'm a-pinin'," many had "pined" for a "sweet kiss" from Salomy Jane, which she had yielded in a sense of honor and fair play. She had never been kissed like this before—she would never again; and yet the man was alive! And behold, she could see in the mirror that she was blushing!

She should hardly know him again. A young man with very bright eyes, a flushed and sunburnt cheek, a kind of fixed look in the face, and no beard; no, none that she could feel. Yet he was not at all like Reuben, not a bit. She took Reuben's picture from the window, and laid it on her workbox. And to think she did not even know this young man's name! That was queer. To be kissed by a man whom she might never know! Of course he knew hers. She wondered if he remembered it and her. But of course he was so glad to get off with his life that he never thought of anything else. Yet she did not give more than four or five minutes to these speculations, and, like a sensible girl, thought of something else. Once again, however, in opening the closet, she found the brown holland gown she had worn on the day before; thought it very unbecoming, and regretted that she had not worn her best gown on her visit to Red Pete's cottage. On such an occasion she really might have been more impressive.

When her father came home that night she asked him the news. No, they had NOT captured the second horse-thief, who was still at large. Judge Boompointer talked of invoking the aid of the despised law. It remained, then, to see whether the horse-thief was fool enough to try to get rid of the animal. Red Pete's body had been delivered to his widow. Perhaps it would only be neighborly for Salomy Jane to ride over to the funeral. But Salomy Jane did not take to the suggestion kindly, nor yet did she explain to her father that, as the other man was still living, she did not care to undergo a second disciplining at the widow's hands. Nevertheless, she contrasted her situation with that of the widow with a new and singular satisfaction. It might have been Red Pete who had escaped. But he had not the grit of the nameless one. She had already settled his heroic quality.

"Ye ain't harkenin' to me, Salomy."

Salomy Jane started.

"Here I'm askin' ye if ye've see that hound Phil Larrabee sneaking by yer today?"

Salomy Jane had not. But she became interested and self-reproachful, for she knew that Phil Larrabee was one of her father's enemies. "He wouldn't dare to go by here unless he knew you were out," she said quickly.

"That's what gets me," he said, scratching his grizzled head. "I've been kind o' thinkin' o' him all day, and one of them Chinamen said he saw him at Sawyer's Crossing. He was a kind of friend o' Pete's wife. That's why I thought yer might find out ef he'd been there." Salomy Jane grew more self-reproachful at her father's self-interest in her "neighborliness." "But that ain't all," continued Mr. Clay. "Thar was tracks over the far pasture that warn't mine. I followed them, and they went round and round the house two or three times, ez ef they mout hev bin prowlin', and then I lost 'em in the woods again. It's just like that sneakin' hound Larrabee to hev bin lyin' in wait for me and afraid to meet a man fair and square in the open."

"You just lie low, dad, for a day or two more, and let me do a little prowlin'," said the girl, with sympathetic indignation in her dark eyes. "Ef it's that skunk, I'll spot him soon enough and let you know whar he's hiding."

"You'll just stay where ye are, Salomy," said her father decisively. "This ain't no woman's work—though I ain't sayin' you haven't got more head for it than some men I know."

Nevertheless, that night, after her father had gone to bed, Salomy Jane sat by the open window of the sitting-room in an apparent attitude of languid contemplation, but alert and intent of eye and ear. It was a fine moonlit night. Two pines near the door, solitary pickets of the serried ranks of distant forest, cast long shadows like paths to the cottage, and sighed their spiced breath in the windows. For there was no frivolity of vine or flower round Salomy Jane's bower. The clearing was too recent, the life too practical for vanities like these. But the moon added a vague elusiveness to everything, softened the rigid outlines of the sheds, gave shadows to the lidless windows, and touched with merciful indirectness the hideous debris of refuse gravel and the gaunt scars of burnt vegetation before the door. Even Salomy Jane was affected by it, and exhaled something between a sigh and a yawn with the breath of the pines. Then she suddenly sat upright.

Her quick ear had caught a faint "click, click," in the direction of the wood; her quicker instinct and rustic training enabled her to determine that it was the ring of a horse's shoe on flinty ground; her knowledge of the locality told her it came from the spot where the trail passed over an outcrop of flint scarcely a quarter of a mile from where she sat, and within the clearing. It was no errant "stock," for the foot was shod with iron; it was a mounted trespasser by night, and boded no good to a man like Clay.

She rose, threw her shawl over her head, more for disguise than shelter, and passed out of the door. A sudden impulse made her seize her father's shotgun from the corner where it stood,—not that she feared any danger to herself, but that it was an excuse. She made directly for the wood, keeping in the shadow of the pines as long as she could. At the fringe she halted; whoever was there must pass her before reaching the house.

Then there seemed to be a suspense of all nature. Everything was deadly still—even the moonbeams appeared no longer tremulous; soon there was a rustle as of some stealthy animal among the ferns, and then a dismounted man stepped into the moonlight. It was the horse-thief—the man she had kissed!

For a wild moment a strange fancy seized her usually sane

intellect and stirred her temperate blood. The news they had told her was NOT true; he had been hung, and this was his ghost! He looked as white and spirit-like in the moonlight, dressed in the same clothes, as when she saw him last. He had evidently seen her approaching, and moved quickly to meet her. But in his haste he stumbled slightly; she reflected suddenly that ghosts did not stumble, and a feeling of relief came over her. And it was no assassin of her father that had been prowling around—only this unhappy fugitive. A momentary color came into her cheek; her coolness and hardihood returned; it was with a tinge of sauciness in her voice that she said:—

"I reckoned you were a ghost."

"I mout have been," he said, looking at her fixedly; "but I reckon I'd have come back here all the same."

"It's a little riskier comin' back alive," she said, with a levity that died on her lips, for a singular nervousness, half fear and half expectation, was beginning to take the place of her relief of a moment ago. "Then it was YOU who was prowlin' round and makin' tracks in the far pasture?"

"Yes; I came straight here when I got away."

She felt his eyes were burning her, but did not dare to raise her own. "Why," she began, hesitated, and ended vaguely. "HOW did you get here?"

"You helped me!"

"I?"

"Yes. That kiss you gave me put life into me—gave me strength to get away. I swore to myself I'd come back and thank you, alive or dead."

Every word he said she could have anticipated, so plain the situation seemed to her now. And every word he said she knew was the truth. Yet her cool common sense struggled against it.

"What's the use of your escaping, ef you're comin' back here to be ketched again?" she said pertly.

He drew a little nearer to her, but seemed to her the more awkward as she resumed her self-possession. His voice, too, was broken, as if by exhaustion, as he said, catching his breath at intervals:—

"I'll tell you. You did more for me than you think. You made another man o' me. I never had a man, woman, or child do to me what you did. I never had a friend—only a pal like Red Pete, who picked me up 'on shares.' I want to quit this yer— what I'm doin'. I want to begin by doin' the square thing to you"—He stopped, breathed hard, and then said brokenly, "My hoss is over thar, staked out. I want to give him to you. Judge Boompointer will give you a thousand dollars for him. I ain't lyin'; it's God's truth! I saw it on the handbill agin a tree. Take him, and I'll get away afoot. Take him. It's the only thing I can do for you, and I know it don't half pay for what you did. Take it; your father can get a reward for you, if you can't."

Such were the ethics of this strange locality that neither the man who made the offer nor the girl to whom it was made was struck by anything that seemed illogical or indelicate, or at all inconsistent with justice or the horse-thief's real conversion. Salomy Jane nevertheless dissented, from another and weaker reason.

"I don't want your hoss, though I reckon dad might; but you're just starvin'. I'll get suthin'." She turned towards the house.

"Say you'll take the hoss first," he said, grasping her hand. At the touch she felt herself coloring and struggled, expecting perhaps another kiss. But he dropped her hand. She turned again with a saucy gesture, said, "Hol' on; I'll come right back," and slipped away, the mere shadow of a coy and flying nymph in the moonlight, until she reached the house.

Here she not only procured food and whiskey, but added a long dust-coat and hat of her father's to her burden. They would serve as a disguise for him and hide that heroic figure, which she thought everybody must now know as she did. Then she rejoined him breathlessly. But he put the food and whiskey aside.

"Listen," he said; "I've turned the hoss into your corral. You'll find him there in the morning, and no one will know but that he got lost and joined the other hosses."

Then she burst out. "But you—YOU—what will become of you? You'll be ketched!"

"I'll manage to get away," he said in a low voice, "ef—ef"—

"Ef what?" she said tremblingly. "Ef you'll put the heart in me again,—as you did!" he gasped.

She tried to laugh—to move away. She could do neither. Suddenly he caught her in his arms, with a long kiss, which she returned again and again. Then they stood embraced as they had embraced two days before, but no longer the same. For the cool, lazy Salomy Jane had been transformed into another woman—a passionate, clinging savage. Perhaps something of her father's blood had surged within her at that supreme moment. The man stood erect and determined.

"Wot's your name?" she whispered quickly. It was a woman's quickest way of defining her feelings.

"Dart."

"Yer first name?"

"Jack."

"Let me go now, Jack. Lie low in the woods till to-morrow sunup. I'll come again."

He released her. Yet she lingered a moment. "Put on those things," she said, with a sudden happy flash of eyes and teeth, "and lie close till I come." And then she sped away home.

But midway up the distance she felt her feet going slower, and something at her heartstrings seemed to be pulling her back. She stopped, turned, and glanced to where he had been standing. Had she seen him then, she might have returned. But he had disappeared. She gave her first sigh, and then ran quickly again. It must be nearly ten o'clock! It was not very long to morning!

She was within a few steps of her own door, when the sleeping woods and silent air appeared to suddenly awake with a sharp "crack!"

She stopped, paralyzed. Another "crack!" followed, that echoed over to the far corral. She recalled herself instantly and dashed off wildly to the woods again.

As she ran she thought of one thing only. He had been "dogged" by one of his old pursuers and attacked. But there were two shots, and he was unarmed. Suddenly she remembered that she had left her father's gun standing against the tree where they were talking. Thank God! she may again have saved him. She ran to the tree; the gun was gone. She ran hither and thither, dreading at every step to fall upon his lifeless body. A new thought struck her; she ran to the corral. The horse was not there! He must have been able to regain it, and escaped, AFTER the shots had been fired. She drew a long breath of relief, but it was caught up in an apprehension of alarm. Her father, awakened from his sleep by the shots, was hurriedly approaching her.

"What's up now, Salomy Jane?" he demanded excitedly.

"Nothin'," said the girl with an effort. "Nothin', at least, that I can find." She was usually truthful because fearless, and a lie stuck in her throat; but she was no longer fearless, thinking of HIM. "I wasn't abed; so I ran out as soon as I heard the shots fired," she answered in return to his curious gaze.

"And you've hid my gun somewhere where it can't be found," he said reproachfully. "Ef it was that sneak Larrabee, and he fired them shots to lure me out, he might have potted me, without a show, a dozen times in the last five minutes."

She had not thought since of her father's enemy! It might indeed have been he who had attacked Jack. But she made a quick point of the suggestion. "Run in, dad, run in and find the gun; you've got no show out here without it." She seized him by the shoulders from behind, shielding him from the woods, and hurried him, half expostulating, half struggling, to the house.

But there no gun was to be found. It was strange; it must

have been mislaid in some corner! Was he sure he had not left it in the barn? But no matter now. The danger was over; the Larrabee trick had failed; he must go to bed now, and in the morning they would make a search together. At the same time she had inwardly resolved to rise before him and make another search of the wood, and perhaps—fearful joy as she recalled her promise!—find Jack alive and well, awaiting her!

Salomy Jane slept little that night, nor did her father. But towards morning he fell into a tired man's slumber until the sun was well up the horizon. Far different was it with his daughter: she lay with her face to the window, her head half lifted to catch every sound, from the creaking of the sun-warped shingles above her head to the far-off moan of the rising wind in the pine trees. Sometimes she fell into a breathless, half-ecstatic trance, living over every moment of the stolen interview; feeling the fugitive's arm still around her, his kisses on her lips; hearing his whispered voice in her ears—the birth of her new life! This was followed again by a period of agonizing dread—that he might even then be lying, his life ebbing away, in the woods, with her name on his lips, and she resting here inactive, until she half started from her bed to go to his succor. And this went on until a pale opal glow came into the sky, followed by a still paler pink on the summit of the white Sierras, when she rose and hurriedly began to dress. Still so sanguine was her hope of meeting him, that she lingered yet a moment to select the brown holland skirt and yellow sunbonnet she had worn when she first saw him. And she had only seen him twice! Only TWICE! It would be cruel, too cruel, not to see him again!

She crept softly down the stairs, listening to the long-drawn breathing of her father in his bedroom, and then, by the light of a guttering candle, scrawled a note to him, begging him not to trust himself out of the house until she returned from her search, and leaving the note open on the table, swiftly ran out into the growing day.

Three hours afterwards Mr. Madison Clay awoke to the sound of loud knocking. At first this forced itself upon his consciousness as his daughter's regular morning summons, and was responded to by a grunt of recognition and a nestling closer in the blankets. Then he awoke with a start and a muttered oath, remembering the events of last night, and his intention to get up early, and rolled out of bed. Becoming aware by this time that the knocking was at the outer door, and hearing the shout of a familiar voice, he hastily pulled on his boots, his jean trousers, and fastening a single suspender over his shoulder as he clattered downstairs, stood in the lower room. The door was open, and waiting upon the threshold was his kinsman, an old ally in many a blood-feud—Breckenridge Clay!

"You ARE a cool one, Mad!" said the latter in half-admiring indignation.

"What's up?" said the bewildered Madison.

"YOU ought to be, and scootin' out o' this," said Breckenridge grimly. "It's all very well to 'know nothin';' but here Phil Larrabee's friends hev just picked him up, drilled through with slugs and deader nor a crow, and now they're lettin' loose Larrabee's two half-brothers on you. And you must go like a derned fool and leave these yer things behind you in the bresh," he went on querulously, lifting Madison Clay's dust-coat, hat, and shotgun from his horse, which stood saddled at the door. "Luckily I picked them up in the woods comin' here. Ye ain't got more than time to get over the state line and among your folks thar afore they'll be down on you. Hustle, old man! What are you gawkin' and starin' at?"

Madison Clay had stared amazed and bewildered—horror-stricken. The incidents of the past night for the first time flashed upon him clearly—hopelessly! The shot; his finding Salomy Jane alone in the woods; her confusion and anxiety to rid herself of him; the disappearance of the shotgun; and now this new discovery of the taking of his hat and coat for a disguise! SHE had killed Phil Larrabee in that disguise, after provoking his first harmless shot! She, his own child, Salomy Jane, had disgraced herself by a man's crime; had disgraced him by usurping his right, and taking a mean advantage, by deceit, of a foe!

"Gimme that gun," he said hoarsely.

Breckenridge handed him the gun in wonder and slowly gathering suspicion. Madison examined nipple and muzzle; one barrel had been discharged. It was true! The gun dropped from his hand.

"Look here, old man," said Breckenridge, with a darkening face, "there's bin no foul play here. Thar's bin no hiring of men, no deputy to do this job. YOU did it fair and square—yourself?"

"Yes, by God!" burst out Madison Clay in a hoarse voice. "Who says I didn't?"

Reassured, yet believing that Madison Clay had nerved himself for the act by an over-draught of whiskey, which had affected his memory, Breckenridge said curtly, "Then wake up and 'lite' out, ef ye want me to stand by you."

"Go to the corral and pick me out a hoss," said Madison slowly, yet not without a certain dignity of manner. "I've suthin' to say to Salomy Jane afore I go." He was holding her scribbled note, which he had just discovered, in his shaking hand.

Struck by his kinsman's manner, and knowing the dependent relations of father and daughter, Breckenridge nodded and hurried away. Left to himself, Madison Clay ran his fingers through his hair, and straightened out the paper on which Salomy Jane had scrawled her note, turned it over, and wrote on the back:—

You might have told me you did it, and not leave your ole father to find it out how you disgraced yourself and him, too, by a low-down, underhanded, woman's trick! I've said I done it, and took the blame myself, and all the sneakiness of it that folks suspect. If I get away alive— and I don't care much which—you needn't foller. The house and stock are yours; but you ain't any longer the daughter of your disgraced father,

MADISON CLAY.

He had scarcely finished the note when, with a clatter of hoofs and a led horse, Breckenridge reappeared at the door elate and triumphant. "You're in nigger luck, Mad! I found that stole hoss of Judge Boompointer's had got away and strayed among your stock in the corral. Take him and you're safe; he can't be outrun this side of the state line."

"I ain't no hoss-thief," said Madison grimly.

"Nobody sez ye are, but you'd be wuss—a fool—ef you didn't take him. I'm testimony that you found him among your hosses; I'll tell Judge Boompointer you've got him, and ye kin send him back when you're safe. The judge will be mighty glad to get him back, and call it quits. So ef you've writ to Salomy Jane, come."

Madison Clay no longer hesitated. Salomy Jane might return at any moment,—it would be part of her "fool womanishness,"—and he was in no mood to see her before a third party. He laid the note on the table, gave a hurried glance around the house, which he grimly believed he was leaving forever, and, striding to the door, leaped on the stolen horse, and swept away with his kinsman.

But that note lay for a week undisturbed on the table in full view of the open door. The house was invaded by leaves, pine cones, birds, and squirrels during the hot, silent, empty days, and at night by shy, stealthy creatures, but never again, day or night, by any of the Clay family. It was known in the district that Clay had flown across the state line, his daughter was believed to have joined him the next day, and the house was supposed to be locked up. It lay off the main road, and few passed that way. The starving cattle in the corral at last broke bounds and spread over the woods. And one night a stronger blast than usual swept through the house, carried the note from the table to the floor, where, whirled into a crack in the flooring, it slowly rotted.

But though the sting of her father's reproach was spared her, Salomy Jane had no need of the letter to know what had happened. For as she entered the woods in the dim light of that morning she saw the figure of Dart gliding from the shadow of a pine towards her. The unaffected cry of joy that rose from her lips died there as she caught sight of his face in the open light.

"You are hurt," she said, clutching his arm passionately.

"No," he said. "But I wouldn't mind that if"—

"You're thinkin' I was afeard to come back last night when I heard the shootin', but I DID come," she went on feverishly. "I ran back here when I heard the two shots, but you were gone. I went to the corral, but your hoss wasn't there, and I thought you'd got away."

"I DID get away," said Dart gloomily. "I killed the man, thinkin' he was huntin' ME, and forgettin' I was disguised. He thought I was your father."

"Yes," said the girl joyfully, "he was after dad, and YOU— you killed him." She again caught his hand admiringly.

But he did not respond. Possibly there were points of honor which this horse-thief felt vaguely with her father. "Listen," he said grimly. "Others think it was your father killed him. When I did it—for he fired at me first—I ran to the corral again and took my hoss, thinkin' I might be follered. I made a clear circuit of the house, and when I found he was the only one, and no one was follerin', I come back here and took off my disguise. Then I heard his friends find him in the wood, and I know they suspected your father. And then another man come through the woods while I was hidin' and found the clothes and took them away." He stopped and stared at her gloomily.

But all this was unintelligible to the girl. "Dad would have got the better of him ef you hadn't," she said eagerly, "so what's the difference?"

"All the same," he said gloomily, "I must take his place."

She did not understand, but turned her head to her master. "Then you'll go back with me and tell him ALL?" she said obediently.

"Yes," he said.

She put her hand in his, and they crept out of the wood together. She foresaw a thousand difficulties, but, chiefest of all, that he did not love as she did. SHE would not have taken these risks against their happiness.

But alas for ethics and heroism. As they were issuing from the wood they heard the sound of galloping hoofs, and had barely time to hide themselves before Madison Clay, on the stolen horse of Judge Boompointer, swept past them with his kinsman.

Salomy Jane turned to her lover.

*****

And here I might, as a moral romancer, pause, leaving the guilty, passionate girl eloped with her disreputable lover, destined to lifelong shame and misery, misunderstood to the last by a criminal, fastidious parent. But I am confronted by certain facts, on which this romance is based. A month later a handbill was posted on one of the sentinel pines, announcing that the property would be sold by auction to the highest bidder by Mrs. John Dart, daughter of Madison Clay, Esq., and it was sold accordingly. Still later—by ten years— the chronicler of these pages visited a certain "stock" or "breeding farm," in the "Blue Grass Country," famous for the popular racers it has produced. He was told that the owner was the "best judge of horse-flesh in the country." "Small wonder," added his informant, "for they say as a young man out in California he was a horse-thief, and only saved himself by eloping with some rich farmer's daughter. But he's a straight-out and respectable man now, whose word about horses can't be bought; and as for his wife, she's a beauty! To see her at the 'Springs,' rigged out in the latest fashion, you'd never think she had ever lived out of New York or wasn't the wife of one of its millionaires."

THE MAN AND THE MOUNTAIN

He was such a large, strong man that, when he first set foot in the little parallelogram I called my garden, it seemed to shrink to half its size and become preposterous. But I noticed at the same time that he was holding in the open palm of his huge hand the roots of a violet, with such infinite tenderness and delicacy that I would have engaged him as my gardener on the spot. But this could not be, as he was already the proud proprietor of a market-garden and nursery on the outskirts of the suburban Californian town where I lived. He would, however, come for two days in the week, stock and look after my garden, and impart to my urban intellect such horticultural hints as were necessary. His name was "Rutli," which I presumed to be German, but which my neighbors rendered as "Rootleigh," possibly from some vague connection with his occupation. His own knowledge of English was oral and phonetic. I have a delightful recollection of a bill of his in which I was charged for "fioletz," with the vague addition of "maine cains." Subsequent explanation proved it to be "many kinds."

Nevertheless, my little garden bourgeoned and blossomed under his large, protecting hand. I became accustomed to walk around his feet respectfully when they blocked the tiny paths, and to expect the total eclipse of that garden-bed on which he worked, by his huge bulk. For the tiniest and most reluctant rootlet seemed to respond to his caressing paternal touch; it was a pretty sight to see his huge fingers tying up some slender stalk to its stick with the smallest thread, and he had a reverent way of laying a bulb or seed in the ground, and then gently shaping and smoothing a small mound over it, which made the little inscription on the stick above more like an affecting epitaph than ever. Much of this gentleness may have been that apology for his great strength, common with large men; but his face was distinctly amiable, and his very light blue eyes were at times wistful and doglike in their kindliness. I was soon to learn, however, that placability was not entirely his nature.

The garden was part of a fifty vara lot of land, on which I was simultaneously erecting a house. But the garden was finished before the house was, through certain circumstances very characteristic of that epoch and civilization. I had purchased the Spanish title, the only LEGAL one, to the land, which, however, had been in POSSESSION of a "squatter." But he had been unable to hold that possession against a "jumper,"—another kind of squatter who had entered upon it covertly, fenced it in, and marked it out in building sites. Neither having legal rights, they could not invoke the law; the last man held possession. There was no doubt that in due course of litigation and time both these ingenuous gentlemen would have been dispossessed in favor of the real owner,—myself,—but that course would be a protracted one. Following the usual custom of the locality, I paid a certain sum to the jumper to yield up peaceably HIS possession of the land, and began to build upon it. It might be reasonably supposed that the question was settled. But it was not. The house was nearly finished when, one morning, I was called out of my editorial sanctum by a pallid painter, looking even more white-leaded than usual, who informed me that my house was in the possession of five armed men! The entry had been made peaceably during the painters' absence to dinner under a wayside tree. When they returned, they had found their pots and brushes in the road, and an intimation from the windows that their reentrance would be forcibly resisted as a trespass.

I honestly believe that Rutli was more concerned than myself over this dispossession. While he loyally believed that I would get back my property, he was dreadfully grieved over the inevitable damage that would be done to the garden during this interval of neglect and carelessness. I even think he would have made a truce with my enemies, if they would only have let him look after his beloved plants. As it was, he kept a passing but melancholy surveillance of them, and was indeed a better spy of the actions of the intruders than any I could have employed. One day, to my astonishment, he brought me a moss-rose bud from a bush which had been trained against a column of the veranda. It appeared that he had called, from over the fence, the attention of one of the men to the neglected condition of the plant, and had obtained permission to "come in and tie it up." The men, being merely hirelings of the chief squatter, had no personal feeling, and I was not therefore surprised to hear that they presently allowed Rutli to come in occasionally and look after his precious "slips." If they had any suspicions of his great strength, it was probably offset by his peaceful avocation and his bland, childlike face. Meantime, I had begun the usual useless legal proceeding, but had also engaged a few rascals of my own to be ready to take advantage of any want of vigilance on the part of my adversaries. I never thought of Rutli in that connection any more than they had.

A few Sundays later I was sitting in the little tea-arbor of Rutli's nursery, peacefully smoking with him. Presently he took his long china-bowled pipe from his mouth, and, looking at me blandly over his yellow mustache, said:—

Bret Harte

"You vonts sometimes to go in dot house, eh?"

I said, "Decidedly."

"Mit a revolver, and keep dot house dose men out?"

"Yes!"

"Vell! I put you in dot house—today!"

"Sunday?"

"Shoost so! It is a goot day! On der Suntay DREE men vill out go to valk mit demselluffs, and visky trinken. TWO," holding up two gigantic fingers, apparently only a shade or two smaller than his destined victims, "stay dere. Dose I lift de fence over."

I hastened to inform him that any violence attempted against the parties WHILE IN POSSESSION, although that possession was illegal, would, by a fatuity of the law, land him in the county jail. I said I would not hear of it.

"But suppose dere vos no fiolence? Suppose dose men vos villin', eh? How vos dot for high?"

"I don't understand."

"So! You shall NOT understand! Dot is better. Go away now and dell your men to coom dot house arount at halluff past dree. But YOU coom, mit yourselluff alone, shoost as if you vos spazieren gehen, for a valk, by dat fence at dree! Ven you shall dot front door vide open see, go in, and dere you vos! You vill der rest leef to me!"

It was in vain that I begged Rutli to divulge his plan, and

pointed out again the danger of his technically breaking the law. But he was firm, assuring me that I myself would be a witness that no assault would be made. I looked into his clear, good-humored eyes, and assented. I had a burning desire to right my wrongs, but I think I also had considerable curiosity.

I passed a miserable quarter of an hour after I had warned my partisans, and then walked alone slowly down the broad leafy street towards the scene of contest. I have a very vivid recollection of my conflicting emotions. I did not believe that I would be killed; I had no distinct intention of killing any of my adversaries; but I had some considerable concern for my loyal friend Rutli, whom I foresaw might be in some peril from the revolver in my unpracticed hand. If I could only avoid shooting HIM, I would be satisfied. I remember that the bells were ringing for church,—a church of which my enemy, the chief squatter, was a deacon in good standing,—and I felt guiltily conscious of my revolver in my hip-pocket, as two or three church-goers passed me with their hymn-books in their hands. I walked leisurely, so as not to attract attention, and to appear at the exact time, a not very easy task in my youthful excitement. At last I reached the front gate with a beating heart. There was no one on the high veranda, which occupied three sides of the low one-storied house, nor in the garden before it. But the front door was open; I softly passed through the gate, darted up the veranda and into the house. A single glance around the hall and bare, deserted rooms, still smelling of paint, showed me it was empty, and with my pistol in one hand and the other on the lock of the door, I stood inside, ready to bolt it against any one but Rutli. But where was HE?

The sound of laughter and a noise like skylarking came from the rear of the house and the back yard. Then I suddenly heard Rutli's heavy tread on the veranda, but it was slow, deliberate, and so exaggerated in its weight that the whole house seemed to shake with it. Then from the window I beheld an extraordinary sight! It was Rutli, swaying from side to side, but steadily carrying with outstretched arms two of the squatter party, his hands tightly grasping their collars. Yet I believe his touch was as gentle as with the violets. His face was preternaturally grave; theirs, to my intense astonishment, while they hung passive from his arms, wore that fatuous, imbecile smile seen on the faces of those who lend themselves to tricks of acrobats and strong men in the arena. He slowly traversed the whole length of one side of the house, walked down the steps to the gate, and then gravely deposited them OUTSIDE. I heard him say, "Dot vins der pet, ain't it?" and immediately after the sharp click of the gate-latch.

Without understanding a thing that had happened, I rightly conceived this was the cue for my appearance with my revolver at the front door. As I opened it I still heard the sound of laughter, which, however, instantly stopped at a sentence from Rutli, which I could not hear. There was an oath, the momentary apparition of two furious and indignant faces over the fence; but these, however, seemed to be instantly extinguished and put down by the enormous palms of Rutli clapped upon their heads. There was a pause, and then Rutli turned around and quietly joined me in the doorway. But the gate was not again opened until the arrival of my partisans, when the house was clearly in my possession.

Safe inside with the door bolted, I turned eagerly to Rutli for an explanation. It then appeared that during his occasional visits to the garden he had often been an object of amusement and criticism to the men on account of his size, which seemed to them ridiculously inconsistent with his great good humor, gentleness, and delicacy of touch. They had doubted his strength and challenged his powers. He had responded once or twice before, lifting weights or even carrying one of his critics at arm's length for a few steps. But he had reserved his final feat for this day and this purpose. It was for a bet, which they had eagerly accepted, secure in their belief in his simplicity, the sincerity of his motives in coming there, and glad of the opportunity of a little Sunday diversion. In their security they had not locked the door when they came out, and had not noticed that HE had opened it. This was his simple story. His only comment, "I haf von der pet, but I dinks I shall nod gollect der money." The two men did not return that afternoon, nor did their comrades. Whether they wisely conceived that a man who was so powerful in play might be terrible in earnest; whether they knew that his act, in which they had been willing performers, had been witnessed by passing citizens, who supposed it was skylarking; or whether their employer got tired of his expensive occupation, I never knew. The public believed the latter; Rutli, myself, and the two men he had evicted alone kept our secret.

From that time Rutli and I became firm friends, and, long after I had no further need of his services in the recaptured house, I often found myself in the little tea-arbor of his prosperous nursery. He was frugal, sober, and industrious; small wonder that in that growing town he waxed rich, and presently opened a restaurant in the main street, connected with his market-garden, which became famous. His relations to me never changed with his changed fortunes; he was always the simple market-gardener and florist who had aided my first housekeeping, and stood by me in an hour of need. Of all things regarding himself he was singularly reticent; I do not think he had any confidants or intimates, even among his own countrymen, whom I believed to be German. But one day he quite accidentally admitted he was a Swiss. As a youthful admirer of the race I was delighted, and told him so, with the enthusiastic addition that I could now quite understand his independence, with his devoted adherence to another's cause. He smiled sadly, and astonished me by saying that he had not heard from Switzerland since he left six years ago. He did not want to hear anything; he even avoided his countrymen lest he should. I was confounded.

"But," I said, "surely you have a longing to return to your country; all Swiss have! You will go back some day just to breathe the air of your native mountains."

"I shall go back some days," said Rutli, "after I have made mooch, mooch money, but not for dot air."

"What for, then?"

"For revenge—to get efen."

Surprised, and for a moment dismayed as I was, I could not help laughing. "Rutli and revenge!" Impossible! And to make it the more absurd, he was still smoking gently and regarding me with soft, complacent eyes. So unchanged was his face and manner that he might have told me he was going back to be married.

"You do not oonderstand," he said forgivingly. "Some days I shall dell to you id. Id is a story. You shall make it yourselluff for dose babers dot you write. It is not bretty, berhaps, ain't it, but it is droo. And de endt is not yet."

Only that Rutli never joked, except in a ponderous fashion with many involved sentences, I should have thought he was taking a good-humored rise out of me. But it was not funny. I am afraid I dismissed it from my mind as a revelation of something weak and puerile, quite inconsistent with his practical common sense and strong simplicity, and wished he had not alluded to it. I never asked him to tell me the story. It was a year later, and only when he had invited me to come to the opening of a new hotel, erected by him at a mountain spa of great resort, that he himself alluded to it.

The hotel was a wonderful affair, even for those days, and Rutli's outlay of capital convinced me that by this time he must have made the "mooch money" he coveted. Something of this was in my mind when we sat by the window of his handsomely furnished private office, overlooking the pines of a Californian canyon. I asked him if the scenery was like Switzerland.

"Ach! no!" he replied; "but I vill puild a hotel shoost like dis dare."

"Is that a part of your revenge?" I asked, with a laugh.

"Ah! so! a bart."

I felt relieved; a revenge so practical did not seem very malicious or idiotic. After a pause he puffed contemplatively at his pipe, and then said, "I dell you somedings of dot story now."

He began. I should like to tell it in his own particular English, mixed with American slang, but it would not convey the simplicity of the narrator. He was the son of a large family who had lived for centuries in one of the highest villages in the Bernese Oberland. He attained his size and strength early, but with a singular distaste to use them in the rough regular work on the farm, although he was a great climber and mountaineer, and, what was at first overlooked as mere boyish fancy, had an insatiable love and curious knowledge of plants and flowers. He knew the haunts of Edelweiss, Alpine rose, and blue gentian, and had brought home rare and unknown blossoms from under the icy lips of glaciers. But as he did this when his time was supposed to be occupied in looking after the cows in the higher pastures and making cheeses, there was trouble in that hard-working, practical family. A giant with the tastes and disposition of a schoolgirl was an anomaly in a Swiss village. Unfortunately again, he was not studious; his record in the village school had been on a par with his manual work, and the family had not even the consolation of believing that they were fostering a genius. In a community where practical industry was the highest virtue, it was not strange, perhaps, that he was called "lazy" and "shiftless;" no one knew the long climbs and tireless vigils he had undergone in remote solitudes in quest of his favorites, or, knowing, forgave him for it. Abstemious, frugal, and patient as he was, even the crusts of his father's table were given him grudgingly. He often went hungry rather than ask the bread he had failed to earn. How his great frame was nurtured in those days he never knew; perhaps the giant mountains recognized some kin in him and fed and strengthened him after their own fashion. Even his gentleness was confounded with cowardice. "Dot vos de hardtest," he said simply; "it is not goot to be opligit to half crush your brudder, ven he would make a laugh of you to your sweetheart." The end came sooner than he expected, and, oddly enough, through this sweetheart. "Gottlieb," she said to him one day, "the English Fremde who stayed here last night met me when I was carrying some of those beautiful flowers you gave me. He asked me where they were to be found, and I told him only YOU knew. He wants to see you; go to him. It may be luck to you." Rutli went. The stranger, an English Alpine climber of scientific tastes, talked with him for an hour. At the end of that time, to everybody's astonishment, he engaged this hopeless idler as his personal guide for three months, at the sum of five francs a day! It was inconceivable, it was unheard of! The Englander was as mad as Gottlieb, whose intellect had always been under suspicion! The schoolmaster pursed up his lips, the pastor shook his head; no good could come of it; the family looked upon it as another freak of Gottlieb's, but there was one big mouth less to feed and more room in the kitchen, and they let him go. They parted from him as ungraciously as they had endured his presence.

Then followed two months of sunshine in Rutli's life—association with his beloved plants, and the intelligent sympathy and direction of a cultivated man. Even in altitudes so dangerous that they had to take other and more experienced guides, Rutli was always at his master's side. That savant's collection of Alpine flora excelled all previous ones; he talked freely with Rutli of further work in the future, and relaxed his English reserve so far as to confide to him that the outcome of their collection and observation might be a book. He gave a flower a Latin name, in which even the ignorant and delighted Rutli could distinguish some likeness to his own. But the book was never compiled. In one of their later and more difficult ascents they and their two additional guides were overtaken by a sudden storm. Swept from their feet down an ice-bound slope, Rutli alone of the roped-together party kept a foothold on the treacherous incline. Here this young Titan, with bleeding fingers clenched in a rock cleft, sustained the struggles and held up the lives of his companions by that precious thread for more than an hour. Perhaps he might have saved them, but in their desperate efforts to regain their footing the rope slipped upon a jagged edge of outcrop and parted as if cut by a knife. The two guides passed without an outcry into obscurity and death; Rutli, with a last despairing exertion, dragged to his own level his unconscious master, crippled by a broken leg.

Your true hero is apt to tell his tale simply. Rutli did not dwell upon these details, nor need I. Left alone upon a treacherous ice slope in benumbing cold, with a helpless man, eight hours afterwards he staggered, half blind, incoherent, and inarticulate, into a "shelter" hut, with the dead body of his master in his stiffened arms. The shelter-keepers turned their attention to Rutli, who needed it most. Blind and delirious, with scarce a chance for life, he was sent the next day to a hospital, where he lay for three months, helpless, imbecile, and unknown. The dead body of the Englishman was identified, and sent home; the bodies of the guides were recovered by their friends; but no one knew aught of Rutli, even his name. While the event was still fresh in the minds of those who saw him enter the hut with the body of his master, a paragraph appeared in a Berne journal recording the heroism of this nameless man. But it could not be corroborated nor explained by the demented hero, and was presently forgotten. Six months from the day he had left his home he was discharged cured. He had not a kreutzer in his pocket; he had never drawn his wages from his employer; he had preferred to have it in a lump sum that he might astonish his family on his return. His eyes were still weak, his memory feeble; only his great physical strength remained through his long illness. A few sympathizing travelers furnished him the means to reach his native village, many miles away. He found his family had heard of the loss of the Englishman and the guides, and had believed he was one of them. Already he was forgotten.

"Ven you vos once peliefed to be det," said Rutli, after a philosophic pause and puff, "it vos not goot to ondeceif beoples. You oopset somedings, soomdimes always. Der hole dot you hef made in der grount, among your frients and your family, vos covered up alretty. You are loocky if you vill not fint some vellars shtanding upon id! My frent, ven you vos DINK det, SHTAY det, BE det, and you vill lif happy!"

"But your sweetheart?" I said eagerly.

A slight gleam of satire stole into Rutli's light eyes. "My sweetheart, ven I vos dinks det, is der miller engaged do bromply! It is mooch better dan to a man dot vos boor and plint and grazy! So! Vell, der next day I pids dem goot-py, und from der door I say, 'I am det now; but ven I next comes pack alife, I shall dis village py! der lants, der houses all togedders. And den for yourselluffs look oudt!'"

"Then that's your revenge? That is what you really intend to do?" I said, half laughing, yet with an uneasy recollection of his illness and enfeebled mind.

"Yes. Look here! I show you somedings." He opened a drawer of his desk and took out what appeared to be some diagrams, plans, and a small water-colored map, like a surveyor's tracing. "Look," he said, laying his finger on the latter, "dat is a map from my fillage. I hef myselluff made it out from my memory. Dot," pointing to a blank space, "is der mountain side high up, so far. It is no goot until I vill a tunnel make or der grade lefel. Dere vas mine fader's house, dere vos der church, der schoolhouse, dot vos de burgomaster's house," he went on, pointing to the respective plots in this old curving parallelogram of the mountain shelf. "So was the fillage when I leave him on the 5th of March, eighteen hundred and feefty. Now you shall see him shoost as I vill make him ven I go back." He took up another plan, beautifully drawn and colored, and evidently done by a professional hand. It was a practical, yet almost fairylike transformation of the same spot! The narrow mountain shelf was widened by excavation, and a boulevard stretched on either side. A great hotel, not unlike the one in which we sat, stood in an open terrace, with gardens and fountains—the site of his father's house. Blocks of pretty dwellings, shops, and cafes filled the intermediate space. I laid down the paper.

"How long have you had this idea?"

"Efer since I left dere, fifteen years ago."

"But your father and mother may be dead by this time?"

"So, but dere vill be odders. Und der blace—it vill remain."

"But all this will cost a fortune, and you are not sure"—

"I know shoost vot id vill gost, to a cend."

"And you think you can ever afford to carry out your idea?"

"I VILL affort id. Ven you shall make yet some moneys and go to Europe, you shall see. I VILL infite you dere first. Now coom and look der house around."

*****

I did NOT make "some moneys," but I DID go to Europe. Three years after this last interview with Rutli I was coming from Interlaken to Berne by rail. I had not heard from him, and I had forgotten the name of his village, but as I looked up from the paper I was reading, I suddenly recognized him in the further end of the same compartment I occupied. His recognition of me was evidently as sudden and unexpected. After our first hand-grasp and greeting, I said:—

"And how about our new village?"

"Dere is no fillage."

"What! You have given up the idea?"

"Yes. There is no fillage, olt or new."

"I don't understand."

He looked at me a moment. "You have not heard?"

"No."

He gently picked up a little local guidebook that lay in my lap, and turning its leaves, pointed to a page, and read as follows:—

"5 M. beyond, the train passes a curve R., where a fine view of the lake may be seen. A little to the R. rises the steep slopes of the—, the scene of a terrible disaster. At three o'clock on March 5, 1850, the little village of—, lying midway of the slope, with its population of 950 souls, was completely destroyed by a landslip from the top of the mountain. So sudden was the catastrophe that not a single escape is recorded. A large portion of the mountain crest, as will be observed when it is seen in profile, descended to the valley, burying the unfortunate village to a depth variously estimated at from 1000 ft. to 1800 ft. The geological causes which produced this extraordinary displacement have been fully discussed, but the greater evidence points to the theory of subterranean glaciers. 5 M. beyond—the train crosses the R. bridge."

I laid down the guide-book in breathless astonishment.

"And you never heard of this in all these years?"

"Nefer! I asked no questions, I read no pooks. I have no ledders from home."

"And yet you"—I stopped, I could not call him a fool; neither could I, in the face of his perfect composure and undisturbed eyes, exhibit a concern greater than his own. An uneasy recollection of what he confessed had been his mental condition immediately after his accident came over me. Had he been the victim of a strange hallucination regarding his house and family all these years? Were these dreams of revenge, this fancy of creating a new village, only an outcome of some shock arising out of the disaster itself, which he had long since forgotten?

He was looking from the window. "Coom," he said, "ve are near der blace. I vill show id to you." He rose and passed out to the rear platform. We were in the rear car, and a new panorama of the lake and mountains flashed upon us at every curve of the line. I followed him. Presently he pointed to what appeared to be a sheer wall of rock and stunted vegetation towering two or three thousand feet above us, which started out of a gorge we were passing. "Dere it vos!" he said. I saw the vast stretch of rock face rising upward and onward, but nothing else. No debris, no ruins, nor even a swelling or rounding of the mountain flank over that awful tomb. Yet, stay! as we dashed across the gorge, and the face of the mountain shifted, high up, the sky-line was slightly broken as if a few inches, a mere handful, of the crest was crumbled away. And then—both gorge and mountain vanished.

I was still embarrassed and uneasy, and knew not what to say to this man at my side, whose hopes and ambition had been as quickly overthrown and buried, and whose life-dream had as quickly vanished. But he himself, taking his pipe from his lips, broke the silence.

"It vos a narrow esgabe!"

"What was?"

"Vy, dis dings. If I had stayed in my fader's house, I vould haf been det for goot, and perried too! Somedimes dose dings cooms oudt apout right, don't id?"

Unvanquished philosopher! As we stood there looking at the flying landscape and sinking lesser hills, one by one the great snow peaks slowly arose behind them, lifting themselves, as if to take a last wondering look at the man they had triumphed over, but had not subdued.

THE PASSING OF ENRIQUEZ

When Enriquez Saltillo ran away with Miss Mannersley, as already recorded in these chronicles,* her relatives and friends found it much easier to forgive that ill-assorted union than to understand it. For, after all, Enriquez was the scion of an old Spanish-Californian family, and in due time would have his share of his father's three square leagues, whatever incongruity there was between his lively Latin extravagance and Miss Mannersley's Puritan precision and intellectual superiority. They had gone to Mexico; Mrs. Saltillo, as was known, having an interest in Aztec antiquities, and he being utterly submissive to her wishes. For myself from my knowledge of Enriquez's nature, I had grave doubts of his entire subjugation, although I knew the prevailing opinion was that Mrs. Saltillo's superiority would speedily tame him. Since his brief and characteristic note apprising me of his marriage, I had not heard from him. It was, therefore, with some surprise, a good deal of reminiscent affection, and a slight twinge of reproach that, two years after, I looked up from some proofs, in the sanctum of the "Daily Excelsior," to recognize his handwriting on a note that was handed to me by a yellow Mexican boy.

* See "The Devotion of Enriquez," in Selected Stories by Bret Harte Gutenberg #1312.

A single glance at its contents showed me that Mrs. Saltillo's correct Bostonian speech had not yet subdued Enriquez's peculiar Spanish-American slang:—

"Here we are again,—right side up with care,—at 1110 Dupont Street, Telegraph Hill. Second floor from top. 'Ring and push.' 'No book agents need apply.' How's your royal nibs? I kiss your hand! Come at six,—the band shall play at seven,—and regard your friend 'Mees Boston,' who will tell you about the little old nigger boys, and your old Uncle 'Ennery."

Two things struck me: Enriquez had not changed; Mrs. Saltillo had certainly yielded up some of her peculiar prejudices. For the address given, far from being a fashionable district, was known as the "Spanish quarter," which, while it still held some old Spanish families, was chiefly given over to half-castes and obscurer foreigners. Even poverty could not have driven Mrs. Saltillo to such a refuge against her will; nevertheless, a good deal of concern for Enriquez's fortune mingled with my curiosity, as I impatiently waited for six o'clock to satisfy it.

It was a breezy climb to 1110 Dupont Street; and although the street had been graded, the houses retained their airy elevation, and were accessible only by successive flights of wooden steps to the front door, which still gave perilously upon the street, sixty feet below. I now painfully appreciated Enriquez's adaptation of the time-honored joke about the second floor. An invincible smell of garlic almost took my remaining breath away as the door was opened to me by a swarthy Mexican woman, whose loose camisa seemed to be slipping from her unstable bust, and was held on only by the mantua-like shawl which supplemented it, gripped by one brown hand. Dizzy from my ascent to that narrow perch, which looked upon nothing but the distant bay and shores of

Contra Costa, I felt as apologetic as if I had landed from a balloon; but the woman greeted me with a languid Spanish smile and a lazy display of white teeth, as if my arrival was quite natural. Don Enriquez, "of a fact," was not himself in the casa, but was expected "on the instant." "Donna Urania" was at home.

"Donna Urania"? For an instant I had forgotten that Mrs. Saltillo's first name was Urania, so pleasantly and spontaneously did it fall from the Spanish lips. Nor was I displeased at this chance of learning something of Don Enriquez's fortunes and the Saltillo menage before confronting my old friend. The servant preceded me to the next floor, and, opening a door, ushered me into the lady's presence.

I had carried with me, on that upward climb, a lively recollection of Miss Mannersley as I had known her two years before. I remembered her upright, almost stiff, slight figure, the graceful precision of her poses, the faultless symmetry and taste of her dress, and the atmosphere of a fastidious and wholesome cleanliness which exhaled from her. In the lady I saw before me, half reclining in a rocking-chair, there was none of the stiffness and nicety. Habited in a loose gown of some easy, flexible, but rich material, worn with that peculiarly indolent slouch of the Mexican woman, Mrs. Saltillo had parted with half her individuality. Even her arched feet and thin ankles, the close-fitting boots or small slippers of which were wont to accent their delicacy, were now lost in a short, low-quartered kid shoe of the Spanish type, in which they moved loosely. Her hair, which she had always worn with a certain Greek simplicity, was parted at one side. Yet her face, with its regularity of feature, and small, thin, red-lipped mouth, was quite unchanged; and her velvety brown eyes were as beautiful and inscrutable as ever.

With the same glance I had taken in her surroundings, quite

as incongruous to her former habits. The furniture, though of old and heavy mahogany, had suffered from careless alien hands, and was interspersed with modern and unmatchable makeshifts, yet preserving the distinctly scant and formal attitude of furnished lodgings. It was certainly unlike the artistic trifles and delicate refinements of her uncle's drawing-room, which we all knew her taste had dictated and ruled. The black and white engravings, the outlined heads of Minerva and Diana, were excluded from the walls for two cheap colored Catholic prints,—a soulless Virgin, and the mystery of the Bleeding Heart. Against the wall, in one corner, hung the only object which seemed a memento of their travels,—a singular-looking upright Indian "papoose-case" or cradle, glaringly decorated with beads and paint, probably an Aztec relic. On a round table, the velvet cover of which showed marks of usage and abusage, there were scattered books and writing materials; and my editorial instinct suddenly recognized, with a thrill of apprehension, the loose leaves of an undoubted manuscript. This circumstance, taken with the fact of Donna Urania's hair being parted on one side, and the general negligee of her appearance, was a disturbing revelation.

My wandering eye apparently struck her, for after the first greeting she pointed to the manuscript with a smile.

"Yes; that is THE manuscript. I suppose Enriquez told you all about it? He said he had written."

I was dumfounded. I certainly had not understood ALL of Enriquez's slang; it was always so decidedly his own, and peculiar. Yet I could not recall any allusion to this.

"He told me something of it, but very vaguely," I ventured to say deprecatingly; "but I am afraid that I thought more of seeing my old friend again than of anything else."

"During our stay in Mexico," continued Mrs. Saltillo, with something of her old precision, "I made some researches into Aztec history, a subject always deeply interesting to me, and I thought I would utilize the result by throwing it on paper. Of course it is better fitted for a volume of reference than for a newspaper, but Enriquez thought you might want to use it for your journal."

I knew that Enriquez had no taste for literature, and had even rather depreciated it in the old days, with his usual extravagance; but I managed to say very pleasantly that I was delighted with his suggestion and should be glad to read the manuscript. After all, it was not improbable that Mrs. Saltillo, who was educated and intelligent, should write well, if not popularly. "Then Enriquez does not begrudge you the time that your work takes from him," I added laughingly. "You seem to have occupied your honeymoon practically."

"We quite comprehend our respective duties," said Mrs. Saltillo dryly; "and have from the first. We have our own lives to live, independent of my uncle and Enriquez's father. We have not only accepted the responsibility of our own actions, but we both feel the higher privilege of creating our own conditions without extraneous aid from our relatives."

It struck me that this somewhat exalted statement was decidedly a pose, or a return of Urania Mannersley's old ironical style. I looked quietly into her brown, near-sighted eyes; but, as once before, my glance seemed to slip from their moist surface without penetrating the inner thought beneath. "And what does Enriquez do for HIS part?" I asked smilingly.

I fully expected to hear that the energetic Enriquez was utilizing his peculiar tastes and experiences by horse-breaking, stock-raising, professional bull-fighting, or even horse-racing, but was quite astonished when she answered quietly:—

"Enriquez is giving himself up to geology and practical metallurgy, with a view to scientific, purely scientific, mining."

Enriquez and geology! In that instant all I could remember of it were his gibes at the "geologian," as he was wont to term Professor Dobbs, a former admirer of Miss Mannersley's. To add to my confusion Mrs. Saltillo at the same moment absolutely voiced my thought.

"You may remember Professor Dobbs," she went on calmly, "one of the most eminent scientists over here, and a very old Boston friend. He has taken Enriquez in hand. His progress is most satisfactory; we have the greatest hopes of him."

"And how soon do you both hope to have some practical results of his study?" I could not help asking a little mischievously; for I somehow resented the plural pronoun in her last sentence.

"Very soon," said Mrs. Saltillo, ignoring everything but the question. "You know Enriquez's sanguine temperament. Perhaps he is already given to evolving theories without a sufficient basis of fact. Still, he has the daring of a discoverer. His ideas of the oolitic formation are not without originality, and Professor Dobbs says that in his conception of the Silurian beach there are gleams that are distinctly precious."

I looked at Mrs. Saltillo, who had reinforced her eyes with her old piquant pince-nez, but could detect no irony in them. She was prettily imperturbable, that was all. There was an awkward silence. Then it was broken by a bounding step on the stairs, a wide-open fling of the door, and Enriquez pirouetted into the room: Enriquez, as of old, unchanged from the crown of his smooth, coal-black hair to the tips of his small, narrow Arabian feet; Enriquez, with his thin, curling mustache, his dancing eyes set in his immovable face, just as I had always known him!

He affected to lapse against the door for a minute, as if staggered by a resplendent vision. Then he said:—

"What do I regard? Is it a dream, or have I again got them—thees jimjams? My best friend and my best—I mean my ONLY—wife! Embrace me!"

He gave me an enthusiastic embrace and a wink like sheet-lightning, passed quickly to his wife, before whom he dropped on one knee, raised the toe of her slipper to his lips, and then sank on the sofa in simulated collapse, murmuring, "Thees is too mooch of white stone for one day!"

Through all this I saw his wife regarding him with exactly the same critically amused expression with which she had looked upon him in the days of their strange courtship. She evidently had not tired of his extravagance, and yet I feel as puzzled by her manner as then. She rose and said: "I suppose you have a good deal to say to each other, and I will leave you by yourselves." Turning to her husband, she added, "I have already spoken about the Aztec manuscript."

The word brought Enriquez to his feet again. "Ah! The little old nigger—you have read?" I began to understand. "My wife, my best friend, and the little old nigger, all in one day. Eet is perfect!" Nevertheless, in spite of this ecstatic and overpowering combination, he hurried to take his wife's hand; kissing it, he led her to a door opening into another room, made her a low bow to the ground as she passed out, and then rejoined me.

"So these are the little old niggers you spoke of in your note," I said, pointing to the manuscript. "Deuce take me if I understood you!"

"Ah, my leetle brother, it is YOU who have changed!" said Enriquez dolorously. "Is it that you no more understand American, or have the 'big head' of the editor? Regard me! Of these Aztecs my wife have made study. She have pursued the little nigger to his cave, his grotto, where he is dead a thousand year. I have myself assist, though I like it not, because thees mummy, look you, Pancho, is not lively. And the mummy who is not dead, believe me! even the young lady mummy, you shall not take to your heart. But my wife"—he stopped, and kissed his hand toward the door whence she had flitted—"ah, SHE is wonderful! She has made the story of them, the peecture of them, from the life and on the instant! You shall take them, my leetle brother, for your journal; you shall announce in the big letter: 'Mooch Importance. The Aztec, He is Found.' 'How He Look and Lif.' 'The Everlasting Nigger.' You shall sell many paper, and Urania shall have scoop in much spondulics and rocks. Hoop-la! For—you comprehend?—my wife and I have settled that she shall forgif her oncle; I shall forgif my father; but from them we take no cent, not a red, not a scad! We are independent! Of ourselves we make a Fourth of July. United we stand; divided we shall fall over! There you are! Bueno!"

It was impossible to resist his wild, yet perfectly sincere, extravagance, his dancing black eyes and occasional flash of white teeth in his otherwise immovable and serious countenance. Nevertheless, I managed to say:—

"But how about yourself, Enriquez, and this geology, you know?"

His eyes twinkled. "Ah, you shall hear. But first you shall take a drink. I have the very old Bourbon. He is not so old as the Aztec, but, believe me, he is very much liflier. Attend! Hol' on!" He was already rummaging on a shelf, but apparently without success; then he explored a buffet, with no better results, and finally attacked a large drawer, throwing out on the floor, with his old impetuosity, a number of geological specimens, carefully labeled. I picked up one that had rolled near me. It was labeled "Conglomerate sandstone." I picked up another: it had the same label.

"Then you are really collecting?" I said, with astonishment.

"Ciertamente," responded Enriquez,—"what other fool shall I look? I shall relate of this geology when I shall have found this beast of a bottle. Ah, here he have hide!" He extracted from a drawer a bottle nearly full of spirits,—tippling was not one of Enriquez's vices. "You shall say 'when.' 'Ere's to our noble selfs!"

When he had drunk, I picked up another fragment of his collection. It had the same label. "You are very rich in 'conglomerate sandstone,'" I said. "Where do you find it?"

"In the street," said Enriquez, with great calmness.

"In the street?" I echoed.

"Yes, my friend! He ees call the 'cobblestone,' also the 'pouding-stone,' when he ees at his home in the country. He ees also a small 'boulder.' I pick him up; I crack him; he made three separate piece of conglomerate sandstone. I bring him home to my wife in my pocket. She rejoice; we are happy. When comes the efening, I sit down and make him a label; while my wife, she sit down and write of the Aztec. Ah, my friend, you shall say of the geology it ees a fine, a

BEAUTIFUL study; but the study of the wife, and what shall please her, believe me, ees much finer! Believe your old Uncle 'Ennery every time! On thees question he gets there; he gets left, nevarre!"

"But Professor Dobbs, your geologian, what does HE say to this frequent recurrence of the conglomerate sandstone period in your study?" I asked quickly.

"He say nothing. You comprehend? He ees a profound geologian, but he also has the admiration excessif for my wife Urania." He stopped to kiss his hand again toward the door, and lighted a cigarette. "The geologian would not that he should break up the happy efening of his friends by thees small detail. He put aside his head—so; he say, 'A leetle freestone, a leetle granite, now and then, for variety; they are building in Montgomery Street.' I take the hint, like a wink to the horse that has gone blind. I attach to myself part of the edifice that is erecting himself in Montgomery Street. I crack him; I bring him home. I sit again at the feet of my beautiful Urania, and I label him 'Freestone,' 'Granite;' but I do not say 'from Parrott's Bank'—eet is not necessary for our happiness."

"And you do this sort of thing only because you think it pleases your wife?" I asked bluntly.

"My friend," rejoined Enriquez, perching himself on the back of the sofa, and caressing his knees as he puffed his cigarette meditatively, "you have ask a conundrum. Gif to me an easier one! It is of truth that I make much of these thing to please Urania. But I shall confess all. Behold, I appear to you, my leetle brother, in my camisa—my shirt! I blow on myself; I gif myself away."

He rose gravely from the sofa, and drew a small box from

one of the drawers of the wardrobe. Opening it, he discovered several specimens of gold-bearing quartz, and one or two scales of gold. "Thees," he said, "friend Pancho, is my own geology; for thees I am what you see. But I say nothing to Urania; for she have much disgust of mere gold,—of what she calls 'vulgar mining,'—and believe me, a fear of the effect of 'speculation' upon my temperamento—you comprehend my complexion, my brother? Reflect upon it, Pancho! I, who am the filosofo, if that I am anything!" He looked at me with great levity of eye and supernatural gravity of demeanor. "But eet ees the jealous affection of the wife, my friend, for which I make play to her with the humble leetle pouding-stone rather than the gold quartz that affrights."

"But what do you want with them, if you have no shares in anything and do not speculate?" I asked.

"Pardon! That ees where you slip up, my leetle friend." He took from the same drawer a clasped portfolio, and unlocked it, producing half a dozen prospectuses and certificates of mining shares. I stood aghast as I recognized the names of one or two extravagant failures of the last ten years,— "played-out" mines that had been galvanized into deceptive life in London, Paris, and New York, to the grief of shareholders abroad and the laughter of the initiated at home. I could scarcely keep my equanimity. "You do not mean to say that you have any belief or interest in this rubbish?" I said quickly.

"What you call 'rubbish,' my good Pancho, ees the rubbish that the American speculator have dump himself upon them in the shaft, the rubbish of the advertisement, of the extravagant expense, of the salary, of the assessment, of the 'freeze-out.' For thees, look you, is the old Mexican mine. My grandfather and hees father have both seen them work before you were born, and the American knew not there was gold in California."

I knew he spoke truly. One or two were original silver mines in the south, worked by peons and Indian slaves, a rope windlass, and a venerable donkey.

"But those were silver mines," I said suspiciously, "and these are gold specimens."

"They are from the same mother," said the imperturbable Enriquez,—"the same mine. The old peons worked him for SILVER, the precious dollar that buy everything, that he send in the galleon to the Philippines for the silk and spice! THAT is good enough for HIM! For the gold he made nothing, even as my leetle wife Urania. And regard me here! There ees a proverb of my father's which say that 'it shall take a gold mine to work a silver mine,' so mooch more he cost. You work him, you are lost! Naturalmente, if you turn him round, if it take you only a silver mine to work a gold mine, you are gain. Thees ees logic!"

The intense gravity of his face at this extraordinary deduction upset my own. But as I was never certain that Enriquez was not purposely mystifying me, with some ulterior object, I could not help saying a little wickedly:—

"Yes, I understand all that; but how about this geologian? Will he not tell your wife? You know he was a great admirer of hers."

"That shall show the great intelligence of him, my Pancho. He will have the four S's,' especially the secreto!"

There could be no serious discussion in his present mood. I gathered up the pages of his wife's manuscript, said lightly that, as she had the first claim upon my time, I should examine the Aztec material and report in a day or two. As I knew I had little chance in the hands of these two incomprehensibles together, I begged him not to call his wife, but to convey my adieus to her, and, in spite of his embraces and protestations, I managed to get out of the room. But I had scarcely reached the front door when I heard Enriquez's voice and his bounding step on the stairs. In another moment his arm was round my neck.

"You must return on the instant! Mother of God! I haf forget, SHE haf forget, WE all haf forget! But you have not seen him!"

"Seen whom?"

"El nino, the baby! You comprehend, pig! The criaturica, the leetle child of ourselfs!"

"The baby?" I said confusedly. "IS there—is there a BABY?"

"You hear him?" said Enriquez, sending an appealing voice upward. "You hear him, Urania? You comprehend. This beast of a leetle brother demands if there ees one!"

"I beg your pardon," I said, hurriedly reascending the stairs. On the landing I met Mrs. Saltillo, but as calm, composed, and precise as her husband was extravagant and vehement. "It was an oversight of Enriquez's," she said quietly, reentering the room with us; "and was all the more strange, as the child was in the room with you all the time."

She pointed to the corner of the wall, where hung what I had believed to be an old Indian relic. To my consternation, it WAS a bark "papoose-case," occupied by a LIVING child, swathed and bandaged after the approved Indian fashion. It was asleep, I believe, but it opened a pair of bright huckleberry eyes, set in the smallest of features, that were like those of a carved ivory idol, and uttered a "coo" at the sound of its mother's voice. She stood on one side with unruffled composure, while Enriquez threw himself into an attitude before it, with clasped hands, as if it had been an image of the Holy Child. For myself, I was too astounded to speak; luckily, my confusion was attributed to the inexperience of a bachelor.

"I have adopted," said Mrs. Saltillo, with the faintest touch of maternal pride in her manner, "what I am convinced is the only natural and hygienic mode of treating the human child. It may be said to be a reversion to the aborigine, but I have yet to learn that it is not superior to our civilized custom. By these bandages the limbs of the infant are kept in proper position until they are strong enough to support the body, and such a thing as malformation is unknown. It is protected by its cradle, which takes the place of its incubating-shell, from external injury, the injudicious coddling of nurses, the so-called 'dancings' and pernicious rockings. The supine position, as in the adult, is imposed only at night. By the aid of this strap it may be carried on long journeys, either by myself or by Enriquez, who thus shares with me, as he fully recognizes, its equal responsibility and burden."

"It—certainly does not—cry," I stammered.

"Crying," said Mrs. Saltillo, with a curve of her pretty red lip, "is the protest of the child against insanitary and artificial treatment. In its upright, unostentatious cradle it is protected against that injudicious fondling and dangerous promiscuous osculation to which, as an infant in human arms, it is so often subjected. Above all, it is kept from that shameless and mortifying publicity so unjust to the weak and unformed animal. The child repays this consideration by a gratifying silence. It cannot be expected to understand our thoughts, speech, or actions; it cannot participate in our pleasures. Why should it be forced into premature contact with them, merely to feed our vanity or selfishness? Why should we assume our particular parental accident as superior to the common lot? If we do not give our offspring that prominence before our visitors so common to the young wife and husband, it is for that reason solely; and this may account for what seemed the forgetfulness of Enriquez in speaking of it or pointing it out to you. And I think his action in calling you back to see it was somewhat precipitate. As one does not usually introduce an unknown and inferior stranger without some previous introduction, he might have asked you if you wished to see the baby before he recalled you."

I looked from Urania's unfathomable eyes to Enriquez's impenetrable countenance. I might have been equal to either of them alone, but together they were invincible. I looked hopelessly at the baby. With its sharp little eyes and composed face, it certainly was a marvelous miniature of Enriquez. I said so.

"It would be singular if it was not," said Mrs. Saltillo dryly; "and as I believe it is by no means an uncommon fact in human nature, it seems to me strange that people should insist upon it as a discovery. It is an inheritance, however, that in due time progress and science will no doubt interrupt, to the advancement of the human race. I need not say that both Enriquez and myself look forward to it with confident tranquillity."

There was clearly nothing for me to do now but to shake hands again and take my leave. Yet I was so much impressed with the unreality of the whole scene that when I reached the front door I had a strong impulse to return suddenly and fall in upon them in their relaxed and natural attitudes. They could not keep up this pose between themselves; and I half expected to see their laughing faces at the window, as I glanced up before wending my perilous way to the street.

I found Mrs. Saltillo's manuscript well written and, in the narrative parts, even graphic and sparkling. I suppressed some general remarks on the universe, and some correlative theories of existence, as not appertaining particularly to the Aztecs, and as not meeting any unquenchable thirst for information on the part of the readers of the "Daily Excelsior." I even promoted my fair contributor to the position of having been commissioned, at great expense, to make the Mexican journey especially for the "Excelsior." This, with Mrs. Saltillo's somewhat precise preraphaelite drawings and water-colors, vilely reproduced by woodcuts, gave quite a sensational air to her production, which, divided into parts, for two or three days filled a whole page of the paper. I am not aware of any particular service that it did to ethnology; but, as I pointed out in the editorial column, it showed that the people of California were not given over by material greed to the exclusion of intellectual research; and as it was attacked instantly in long communications from one or two scientific men, it thus produced more copy.

Briefly, it was a boom for the author and the "Daily Excelsior." I should add, however, that a rival newspaper intimated that it was also a boom for Mrs. Saitillo's HUSBAND, and called attention to the fact that a deserted Mexican mine, known as "El Bolero," was described graphically in the Aztec article among the news, and again appeared in the advertising columns of the same paper. I turned somewhat indignantly to the file of the "Excelsior," and, singularly enough, found in the elaborate prospectus of a new gold-mining company the description of the El Bolero mine as a QUOTATION from the Aztec article, with extraordinary inducements for the investment of capital in the projected working of an old mine. If I had had any difficulty in recognizing in the extravagant style the flamboyant hand of Enriquez in English writing, I might have read his name plainly enough displayed as president of the company. It was evidently the prospectus of one of the ventures he had shown me. I was more amused than indignant at the little trick he had played upon my editorial astuteness. After all, if I had thus benefited the young couple I was satisfied. I had not seen them since my first visit, as I was very busy,—my communications with Mrs. Saltillo had been carried on by letters and proofs,—and when I did finally call at their house, it was only to find that they were visiting at San Jose. I wondered whether the baby was still hanging on the wall, or, if he was taken with them, who carried him.

A week later the stock of El Bolero was quoted at par. More than that, an incomprehensible activity had been given to all the deserted Mexican mines, and people began to look up scrip hitherto thrown aside as worthless. Whether it was one of those extraordinary fevers which attacked Californian speculation in the early days, or whether Enriquez Saltillo had infected the stock-market with his own extravagance, I never knew; but plans as wild, inventions as fantastic, and arguments as illogical as ever emanated from his own brain, were set forth "on 'Change" with a gravity equal to his own. The most reasonable hypothesis was that it was the effect of the well-known fact that the Spanish Californian hitherto had not been a mining speculator, nor connected in any way with the gold production on his native soil, deeming it inconsistent with his patriarchal life and landed dignity, and that when a "son of one of the oldest Spanish families, identified with the land and its peculiar character for centuries, lent himself to its mineral exploitations,"—I beg to say that I am quoting from the advertisement in the

"Excelsior,"—"it was a guerdon of success." This was so far true that in a week Enriquez Saltillo was rich, and in a fair way to become a millionaire.

It was a hot afternoon when I alighted from the stifling Wingdam coach, and stood upon the cool, deep veranda of the Carquinez Springs Hotel. After I had shaken off the dust which had lazily followed us, in our descent of the mountain road, like a red smoke, occasionally overflowing the coach windows, I went up to the room I had engaged for my brief holiday. I knew the place well, although I could see that the hotel itself had lately been redecorated and enlarged to meet the increasing requirements of fashion. I knew the forest of enormous redwoods where one might lose one's self in a five minutes' walk from the veranda. I knew the rocky trail that climbed the mountain to the springs, twisting between giant boulders. I knew the arid garden, deep in the wayside dust, with its hurriedly planted tropical plants, already withering in the dry autumn sunshine, and washed into fictitious freshness, night and morning by the hydraulic irrigating-hose. I knew, too, the cool, reposeful night winds that swept down from invisible snow-crests beyond, with the hanging out of monstrous stars, that too often failed to bring repose to the feverish guests. For the overstrained neurotic workers who fled hither from the baking plains of Sacramento, or from the chill sea-fogs of San Francisco, never lost the fierce unrest that had driven them here. Unaccustomed to leisure, their enforced idleness impelled them to seek excitement in the wildest gayeties; the bracing mountain air only reinvigorated them to pursue pleasure as they had pursued the occupations they had left behind. Their sole recreations were furious drives over break-neck roads; mad, scampering cavalcades through the sedate woods; gambling parties in private rooms, where large sums were lost by capitalists on leave; champagne suppers; and impromptu balls that lasted through the calm, reposeful night to the first rays of light on the distant snowline. Unimaginative men, in their temporary sojourn they more often outraged or dispossessed nature in her own fastnesses than courted her for sympathy or solitude. There were playing-cards left lying behind boulders, and empty champagne bottles forgotten in forest depths.

I remembered all this when, refreshed by a bath, I leaned from the balcony of my room and watched the pulling up of a brake, drawn by six dusty, foam-bespattered horses, driven by a noted capitalist. As its hot, perspiring, closely veiled yet burning-faced fair occupants descended, in all the dazzling glory of summer toilets, and I saw the gentlemen consult their watches with satisfaction, and congratulate their triumphant driver, I knew the characteristic excitement they had enjoyed from a "record run," probably for a bet, over a mountain road in a burning sun.

"Not bad, eh? Forty-four minutes from the summit!"

The voice seemed at my elbow. I turned quickly, to recognize an acquaintance, a young San Francisco broker, leaning from the next balcony to mine. But my attention was just then preoccupied by the face and figure, which seemed familiar to me, of a woman who was alighting from the brake.

"Who is that?" I asked; "the straight slim woman in gray, with the white veil twisted round her felt hat?"

"Mrs. Saltillo," he answered; "wife of 'El Bolero' Saltillo, don't you know. Mighty pretty woman, if she is a little stiffish and set up."

Then I had not been mistaken! "Is Enriquez—is her husband —here?" I asked quickly.

The man laughed. "I reckon not. This is the place for other people's husbands, don't you know."

Alas! I DID know; and as there flashed upon me all the miserable scandals and gossip connected with this reckless, frivolous caravansary, I felt like resenting his suggestion. But my companion's next words were more significant:—

"Besides, if what they say is true, Saltillo wouldn't be very popular here."

"I don't understand," I said quickly.

"Why, after all that row he had with the El Bolero Company."

"I never heard of any row," I said, in astonishment.

The broker laughed incredulously. "Come! and YOU a newspaper man! Well, maybe they DID try to hush it up, and keep it out of the papers, on account of the stock. But it seems he got up a reg'lar shindy with the board, one day; called 'em thieves and swindlers, and allowed he was disgracing himself as a Spanish hidalgo by having anything to do with 'em. Talked, they say, about Charles V. of Spain, or some other royal galoot, giving his ancestors the land in trust! Clean off his head, I reckon. Then shunted himself off the company, and sold out. You can guess he wouldn't be very popular around here, with Jim Bestley, there," pointing to the capitalist who had driven the brake, "who used to be on the board with him. No, sir. He was either lying low for something, or was off his head. Think of his throwing up a place like that!"

"Nonsense!" I said indignantly. "He is mercurial, and has the quick impulsiveness of his race, but I believe him as sane as any who sat with him on the board. There must be some mistake, or you haven't got the whole story." Nevertheless, I did not care to discuss an old friend with a mere acquaintance, and I felt secretly puzzled to account for his conduct, in the face of his previous cleverness in manipulating the El Bolero, and the undoubted fascination he had previously exercised over the stockholders. The story had, of course, been garbled in repetition. I had never before imagined what might be the effect of Enriquez's peculiar eccentricities upon matter-of-fact people,—I had found them only amusing,—and the broker's suggestion annoyed me. However, Mrs. Saltillo was here in the hotel, and I should, of course, meet her. Would she be as frank with me?

I was disappointed at not finding her in the drawing-room or on the veranda; and the heat being still unusually oppressive, I strolled out toward the redwoods, hesitating for a moment in the shade before I ran the fiery gauntlet of the garden. To my surprise, I had scarcely passed the giant sentinels on its outskirts before I found that, from some unusual condition of the atmosphere, the cold undercurrent of air which generally drew through these pillared aisles was withheld that afternoon; it was absolutely hotter than in the open, and the wood was charged throughout with the acrid spices of the pine. I turned back to the hotel, reascended to my bedroom, and threw myself in an armchair by the open window. My room was near the end of a wing; the corner room at the end was next to mine, on the same landing. Its closed door, at right angles to my open one, gave upon the staircase, but was plainly visible from where I sat. I remembered being glad that it was shut, as it enabled me without offense to keep my own door open.

The house was very quiet. The leaves of a catalpa, across the roadway, hung motionless. Somebody yawned on the veranda below. I threw away my half-finished cigar, and closed my eyes. I think I had not lost consciousness for more than a few seconds before I was awakened by the shaking and thrilling of the whole building. As I staggered to my feet, I saw the four pictures hanging against the wall swing outwardly from it on their cords, and my door swing back against the wall. At the same moment, acted upon by the same potential impulse, the door of the end room in the hall, opposite the stairs, also swung open. In that brief moment I had a glimpse of the interior of the room, of two figures, a man and a woman, the latter clinging to her companion in abject terror. It was only for an instant, for a second thrill passed through the house, the pictures clattered back against the wall, the door of the end room closed violently on its strange revelation, and my own door swung back also. Apprehensive of what might happen, I sprang toward it, but only to arrest it an inch or two before it should shut, when, as my experience had taught me, it might stick by the subsidence of the walls. But it did stick ajar, and remained firmly fixed in that position. From the clattering of the knob of the other door, and the sound of hurried voices behind it, I knew that the same thing had happened there when that door had fully closed.

I was familiar enough with earthquakes to know that, with the second shock or subsidence of the earth, the immediate danger was passed, and so I was able to note more clearly what else was passing. There was the usual sudden stampede of hurrying feet, the solitary oath and scream, the half-hysterical laughter, and silence. Then the tumult was reawakened to the sound of high voices, talking all together, or the impatient calling of absentees in halls and corridors. Then I heard the quick swish of female skirts on the staircase, and one of the fair guests knocked impatiently at the door of the end room, still immovably fixed. At the first knock there was a sudden cessation of the hurried whisperings and turning of the doorknob.

"Mrs. Saltillo, are you there? Are you frightened?" she called.

"Mrs. Saltillo"! It was SHE, then, who was in the room! I drew nearer my door, which was still fixed ajar. Presently a voice,—Mrs. Saltillo's voice,—with a constrained laugh in it, came from behind the door: "Not a bit. I'll come down in a minute."

"Do," persisted the would-be intruder. "It's all over now, but we're all going out into the garden; it's safer."

"All right," answered Mrs. Saltillo. "Don't wait, dear. I'll follow. Run away, now."

The visitor, who was evidently still nervous, was glad to hurry away, and I heard her retreating step on the staircase. The rattling of the door began again, and at last it seemed to yield to a stronger pull, and opened sufficiently to allow Mrs. Saltillo to squeeze through. I withdrew behind my door. I fancied that it creaked as she passed, as if, noticing it ajar, she had laid an inquiring hand upon it. I waited, but she was not followed by any one. I wondered if I had been mistaken. I was going to the bell-rope to summon assistance to move my own door when a sudden instinct withheld me. If there was any one still in that room, he might come from it just as the servant answered my call, and a public discovery would be unavoidable. I was right. In another instant the figure of a man, whose face I could not discern, slipped out of the room, passed my door, and went stealthily down the staircase.

Convinced of this, I resolved not to call public attention to my being in my own room at the time of the incident; so I did not summon any one, but, redoubling my efforts, I at last opened the door sufficiently to pass out, and at once joined the other guests in the garden. Already, with characteristic recklessness and audacity, the earthquake was made light of; the only dictate of prudence had resolved itself into a hilarious proposal to "camp out" in the woods all night, and have a "torch-light picnic." Even then preparations were being made for carrying tents, blankets, and pillows to the adjacent redwoods; dinner and supper, cooked at campfires, were to be served there on stumps of trees and fallen logs. The convulsion of nature had been used as an excuse for one of the wildest freaks of extravagance that Carquinez Springs had ever known. Perhaps that quick sense of humor which dominates the American male in exigencies of this kind kept the extravagances from being merely bizarre and grotesque, and it was presently known that the hotel and its menage were to be appropriately burlesqued by some of the guests, who, attired as Indians, would personate the staff, from the oracular hotel proprietor himself down to the smart hotel clerk.

During these arrangements I had a chance of drawing near Mrs. Saltillo. I fancied she gave a slight start as she recognized me; but her greetings were given with her usual precision. "Have you been here long?" she asked.

"I have only just come," I replied laughingly; "in time for the shock."

"Ah, you felt it, then? I was telling these ladies that our eminent geologist, Professor Dobbs, assured me that these seismic disturbances in California have a very remote centre, and are seldom serious."

"It must be very satisfactory to have the support of geology at such a moment," I could not help saying, though I had not the slightest idea whose the figure was that I had seen, nor, indeed, had I recognized it among the guests. She did not seem to detect any significance in my speech, and I added:

"And where is Enriquez? He would enjoy this proposed picnic to-night."

"Enriquez is at Salvatierra Rancho, which he lately bought from his cousin."

"And the baby? Surely, here is a chance for you to hang him up on a redwood tonight, in his cradle."

"The boy," said Mrs. Saltillo quickly, "is no longer in his cradle; he has passed the pupa state, and is now free to develop his own perfected limbs. He is with his father. I do not approve of children being submitted to the indiscriminate attentions of a hotel. I am here myself only for that supply of ozone indicated for brain exhaustion."

She looked so pretty and prim in her gray dress, so like her old correct self, that I could not think of anything but her mental attitude, which did not, by the way, seem much like mental depression. Yet I was aware that I was getting no information of Enriquez's condition or affairs, unless the whole story told by the broker was an exaggeration. I did not, however, dare to ask more particularly.

"You remember Professor Dobbs?" she asked abruptly.

This recalled a suspicion awakened by my vision, so suddenly that I felt myself blushing. She did not seem to notice it, and was perfectly composed.

"I do remember him. Is he here?"

"He is; that is what makes it so particularly unfortunate for me. You see, after that affair of the board, and Enriquez's withdrawal, although Enriquez may have been a little precipitate in his energetic way, I naturally took my husband's part in public; for although we preserve our own independence inviolable, we believe in absolute confederation as against society."

"But what has Professor Dobbs to do with the board?" I interrupted.

"The professor was scientific and geological adviser to the board, and it was upon some report or suggestion of his that Enriquez took issue, against the sentiment of the board. It was a principle affecting Enriquez's Spanish sense of honor."

"Do tell me all about it," I said eagerly; "I am very anxious to know the truth."

"As I was not present at the time," said Mrs. Saltillo, rebuking my eagerness with a gentle frigidity, "I am unable to do so. Anything else would be mere hearsay, and more or less ex parte. I do not approve of gossip."

"But what did Enriquez tell you? You surely know that."

"THAT, being purely confidential, as between husband and wife,—perhaps I should say partner and partner,—of course you do not expect me to disclose. Enough that I was satisfied with it. I should not have spoken to you about it at all, but that, through myself and Enriquez, you are an acquaintance of the professor's, and I might save you the awkwardness of presenting yourself with him. Otherwise, although you are a friend of Enriquez, it need not affect your acquaintance with the professor."

"Hang the professor!" I ejaculated. "I don't care a rap for HIM."

"Then I differ with you," said Mrs. Saltillo, with precision.

"He is distinctly an able man, and one cannot but miss the contact of his original mind and his liberal teachings."

Here she was joined by one of the ladies, and I lounged away. I dare say it was very mean and very illogical, but the unsatisfactory character of this interview made me revert again to the singular revelation I had seen a few hours before. I looked anxiously for Professor Dobbs; but when I did meet him, with an indifferent nod of recognition, I found I could by no means identify him with the figure of her mysterious companion. And why should I suspect him at all, in the face of Mrs. Saltillo's confessed avoidance of him? Who, then, could it have been? I had seen them but an instant, in the opening and the shutting of a door. It was merely the shadowy bulk of a man that flitted past my door, after all. Could I have imagined the whole thing? Were my perceptive faculties—just aroused from slumber, too insufficiently clear to be relied upon? Would I not have laughed had Urania, or even Enriquez himself, told me such a story?

As I reentered the hotel the clerk handed me a telegram. "There's been a pretty big shake all over the country," he said eagerly. "Everybody is getting news and inquiries from their friends. Anything fresh?" He paused interrogatively as I tore open the envelope. The dispatch had been redirected from the office of the "Daily Excelsior." It was dated, "Salvatierra Rancho," and contained a single line: "Come and see your old uncle 'Ennery."

There was nothing in the wording of the message that was unlike Enriquez's usual light-hearted levity, but the fact that he should have TELEGRAPHED it to me struck me uneasily. That I should have received it at the hotel where his wife and Professor Dobbs were both staying, and where I had had such a singular experience, seemed to me more than a mere coincidence. An instinct that the message was something personal to Enriquez and myself kept me from imparting it to Mrs. Saltillo. After worrying half the night in our bizarre camp in the redwoods, in the midst of a restless festivity which was scarcely the repose I had been seeking at Carquinez Springs, I resolved to leave the next day for Salvatierra Rancho. I remembered the rancho,—a low, golden-brown, adobe-walled quadrangle, sleeping like some monstrous ruminant in a hollow of the Contra Costa Range. I recalled, in the midst of this noisy picnic, the slumberous coolness of its long corridors and soundless courtyard, and hailed it as a relief. The telegram was a sufficient excuse for my abrupt departure. In the morning I left, but without again seeing either Mrs. Saltillo or the professor.

It was late the next afternoon when I rode through the canada that led to the rancho. I confess my thoughts were somewhat gloomy, in spite of my escape from the noisy hotel; but this was due to the sombre scenery through which I had just ridden, and the monotonous russet of the leagues of wild oats. As I approached the rancho, I saw that Enriquez had made no attempt to modernize the old casa, and that even the garden was left in its lawless native luxuriance, while the rude tiled sheds near the walled corral contained the old farming implements, unchanged for a century, even to the ox-carts, the wheels of which were made of a single block of wood. A few peons, in striped shirts and velvet jackets, were sunning themselves against a wall, and near them hung a half-drained pellejo, or goatskin water-bag. The air of absolute shiftlessness must have been repellent to Mrs. Saltillo's orderly precision, and for a moment I pitied her. But it was equally inconsistent with Enriquez's enthusiastic ideas of American progress, and the extravagant designs he had often imparted to me of the improvements he would make when he had a fortune. I was feeling uneasy again, when I suddenly heard the rapid clack of unshod hoofs on a

Bret Harte

rocky trail that joined my own. At the same instant a horseman dashed past me at full speed. I had barely time to swerve my own horse aside to avoid a collision, yet in that brief moment I recognized the figure of Enriquez. But his face I should have scarcely known. It was hard and fixed. His upper lip and thin, penciled mustache were drawn up over his teeth, which were like a white gash in his dark face. He turned into the courtyard of the rancho. I put spurs to my horse, and followed, in nervous expectation. He turned in his saddle as I entered. But the next moment he bounded from his horse, and, before I could dismount, flew to my side and absolutely lifted me from the saddle to embrace me. It was the old Enriquez again; his face seemed to have utterly changed in that brief moment.

"This is all very well, old chap," I said; "but do you know that you nearly ran me down, just now, with that infernal half-broken mustang? Do you usually charge the casa at that speed?"

"Pardon, my leetle brother! But here you shall slip up. The mustang is not HALF-broken; he is not broke at all! Look at his hoof—never have a shoe been there. For myself—attend me! When I ride alone, I think mooch; when I think mooch I think fast; my idea he go like a cannon-ball! Consequent, if I ride not thees horse like the cannon-ball, my thought HE arrive first, and where are you? You get left! Believe me that I fly thees horse, thees old Mexican plug, and your de' uncle 'Ennery and his leetle old idea arrive all the same time, and on the instant."

It WAS the old Enriquez! I perfectly understood his extravagant speech and illustration, and yet for the first time I wondered if others did.

"Tak'-a-drink!" he said, all in one word. "You shall possess the old Bourbon or the rhum from the Santa Cruz! Name your poison, gentlemen!"

He had already dragged me up the steps from the patio to the veranda, and seated me before a small round table still covered with the chocolate equipage of the morning. A little dried-up old Indian woman took it away, and brought the spirits and glasses.

"Mirar the leetle old one!" said Enriquez, with unflinching gravity. "Consider her, Pancho, to the bloosh! She is not truly an Aztec, but she is of years one hundred and one, and LIFS! Possibly she haf not the beauty which ravishes, which devastates. But she shall attent you to the hot water, to the bath. Thus shall you be protect, my leetle brother, from scandal."

"Enriquez," I burst out suddenly, "tell me about yourself. Why did you leave the El Bolero board? What was the row about?"

Enriquez's eyes for a moment glittered; then they danced as before.

"Ah," he said, "you have heard?"

"Something; but I want to know the truth from you."

He lighted a cigarette, lifted himself backward into a grass hammock, on which he sat, swinging his feet. Then, pointing to another hammock, he said: "Tranquillize yourself there. I will relate; but, truly, it ees nothing."

He took a long pull at his cigarette, and for a few moments seemed quietly to exude smoke from his eyes, ears, nose, even his finger-ends—everywhere, in fact, but his mouth.

That and his mustache remained fixed. Then he said slowly, flicking away the ashes with his little finger:—

"First you understand, friend Pancho, that I make no row. The other themself make the row, the shindig. They make the dance, the howl, the snap of the finger, the oath, the 'Helen blazes,' the 'Wot the devil,' the 'That be d—d,' the bad language; they themselves finger the revolver, advance the bowie-knife, throw off the coat, square off, and say 'Come on.' I remain as you see me now, little brother—tranquil." He lighted another cigarette, made his position more comfortable in the hammock, and resumed: "The Professor Dobbs, who is the geologian of the company, made a report for which he got two thousand dollar. But thees report—look you, friend Pancho—he is not good for the mine. For in the hole in the ground the Professor Dobbs have found a 'hoss.'"

"A what?" I asked.

"A hoss," repeated Enriquez, with infinite gravity. "But not, leetle Pancho, the hoss that run, the hoss that buck-jump, but what the miner call a 'hoss,' a something that rear up in the vein and stop him. You pick around the hoss; you pick under him; sometimes you find the vein, sometimes you do not. The hoss rear up, and remain! Eet ees not good for the mine. The board say, 'D—the hoss!' 'Get rid of the hoss.' 'Chuck out the hoss.' Then they talk together, and one say to the Professor Dobbs: 'Eef you cannot thees hoss remove from the mine, you can take him out of the report.' He look to me, thees professor. I see nothing; I remain tranquil. Then the board say: 'Thees report with the hoss in him is worth two thousand dollar, but WITHOUT the hoss he is worth five thousand dollar. For the stockholder is frighted of the rearing hoss. It is of a necessity that the stockholder should remain tranquil. Without the hoss the report is good; the stock shall errise; the director shall sell out, and leave the stockholder the hoss to play with.' The professor he say, 'Al-right;' he scratch out the hoss, sign his name, and get a check for three thousand dollar."

"Then I errise—so!" He got up from the hammock, suiting the action to the word, and during the rest of his narrative, I honestly believe, assumed the same attitude and deliberate intonation he had exhibited at the board. I could even fancy I saw the reckless, cynical faces of his brother directors turned upon his grim, impassive features. "I am tranquil. I smoke my cigarette. I say that for three hundred year my family have held the land of thees mine; that it pass from father to son, and from son to son; it pass by gift, it pass by grant, but that NEVARRE THERE PASS A LIE WITH IT! I say it was a gift by a Spanish Christian king to a Christian hidalgo for the spread of the gospel, and not for the cheat and the swindle! I say that this mine was worked by the slave, and by the mule, by the ass, but never by the cheat and swindler. I say that if they have struck the hoss in the mine, they have struck a hoss IN THE LAND, a Spanish hoss; a hoss that have no bridle worth five thousand dollar in his mouth, but a hoss to rear, and a hoss that cannot be struck out by a Yankee geologian; and that hoss is Enriquez Saltillo!"

He paused, and laid aside his cigarette.

"Then they say, 'Dry up,' and 'Sell out;' and the great bankers say, 'Name your own price for your stock, and resign.' And I say, 'There is not enough gold in your bank, in your San Francisco, in the mines of California, that shall buy a Spanish gentleman. When I leave, I leave the stock at my back; I shall take it, nevarre! Then the banker he say, 'And you will go and blab, I suppose?' And then, Pancho, I smile, I pick up my mustache—so! and I say: 'Pardon, senor, you haf mistake, The Saltillo haf for three hundred year no stain, no blot upon him. Eet is not now—the last of the race—who shall confess that he haf sit at a board of disgrace and dishonor!' And then it is that the band begin to play, and the animals stand on their hind leg and waltz, and behold, the row he haf begin!"

I ran over to him, and fairly hugged him. But he put me aside with a gentle and philosophical calm. "Ah, eet is nothing, Pancho. It is, believe me, all the same a hundred years to come, and where are you, then? The earth he turn round, and then come el temblor, the earthquake, and there you are! Bah! eet is not of the board that I have asked you to come; it is something else I would tell you. Go and wash yourself of thees journey, my leetle brother, as I have"—looking at his narrow, brown, well-bred hands—"wash myself of the board. Be very careful of the leetle old woman, Pancho; do not wink to her of the eye! Consider, my leetle brother, for one hundred and one year he haf been as a nun, a saint! Disturb not her tranquillity."

Yes, it was the old Enriquez; but he seemed graver,—if I could use that word of one of such persistent gravity; only his gravity heretofore had suggested a certain irony rather than a melancholy which I now fancied I detected. And what was this "something else" he was to "tell me later"? Did it refer to Mrs. Saltillo? I had purposely waited for him to speak of her, before I should say anything of my visit to Carquinez Springs. I hurried through my ablutions in the hot water, brought in a bronze jar on the head of the centenarian handmaid; and even while I was smiling over Enriquez's caution regarding this aged Ruth, I felt I was getting nervous to hear his news.

I found him in his sitting-room, or study,—a long, low apartment with small, deep windows like embrasures in the outer adobe wall, but glazed in lightly upon the veranda. He was sitting quite abstractedly, with a pen in his hand, before a table, on which a number of sealed envelopes were lying. He looked SO formal and methodical for Enriquez.

"You like the old casa, Pancho?" he said in reply to my praise of its studious and monastic gloom. "Well, my leetle brother, some day that is fair—who knows?—it may be at your disposicion; not of our politeness, but of a truth, friend Pancho. For, if I leave it to my wife"—it was the first time he had spoken of her—"for my leetle child," he added quickly, "I shall put in a bond, an obligacion, that my friend Pancho shall come and go as he will."

"The Saltillos are a long-lived race," I laughed. "I shall be a gray-haired man, with a house and family of my own by that time." But I did not like the way he had spoken.

"Quien sabe?" he only said, dismissing the question with the national gesture. After a moment he added: "I shall tell you something that is strrange, so strrange that you shall say, like the banker say, 'Thees Enriquez, he ees off his head; he ees a crank, a lunatico;' but it ees a FACT; believe me, I have said!"

He rose, and, going to the end of the room, opened a door. It showed a pretty little room, femininely arranged in Mrs. Saltillo's refined taste. "Eet is pretty; eet is the room of my wife. Bueno! attend me now." He closed the door, and walked back to the table. "I have sit here and write when the earthquake arrive. I have feel the shock, the grind of the walls on themselves, the tremor, the stagger, and—that—door—he swing open!"

"The door?" I said, with a smile that I felt was ghastly.

"Comprehend me," he said quickly; "it ees not THAT which ees strrange. The wall lift, the lock slip, the door he fell open; it is frequent; it comes so ever when the earthquake come. But eet is not my wife's room I see; it is ANOTHER ROOM, a room I know not. My wife Urania, she stand there, of a fear, of a tremble; she grasp, she cling to someone. The earth shake again; the door shut. I jump from my table; I shake and tumble to the door. I fling him open. Maravilloso! it is the room of my wife again. She is NOT there; it is empty; it is nothing!"

I felt myself turning hot and cold by turns. I was horrified, and—and I blundered. "And who was the other figure?" I gasped.

"Who?" repeated Enriquez, with a pause, a fixed look at me, and a sublime gesture. "Who SHOULD it be, but myself, Enriquez Saltillo?"

A terrible premonition that this was a chivalrous LIE, that it was NOT himself he had seen, but that our two visions were identical, came upon me. "After all," I said, with a fixed smile, "if you could imagine you saw your wife, you could easily imagine you saw yourself too. In the shock of the moment you thought of HER naturally, for then she would as naturally seek your protection. You have written for news of her?"

"No," said Enriquez quietly.

"No?" I repeated amazedly.

"You understand, Pancho! Eef it was the trick of my eyes, why should I affright her for the thing that is not? If it is the truth, and it arrive to ME, as a warning, why shall I affright her before it come?"

"Before WHAT comes? What is it a warning of?" I asked impetuously.

"That we shall be separated! That I go, and she do not."

To my surprise, his dancing eyes had a slight film over them. "I don't understand you," I said awkwardly.

"Your head is not of a level, my Pancho. Thees earthquake he remain for only ten seconds, and he fling open the door. If he remain for twenty seconds, he fling open the wall, the hoose toomble, and your friend Enriquez is feenish."

"Nonsense!" I said. "Professor—I mean the geologists—say that the centre of disturbance of these Californian earthquakes is some far-away point in the Pacific and there never will be any serious convulsions here."

"Ah, the geologist," said Enriquez gravely, "understand the hoss that rear in the mine, and the five thousand dollar, believe me, no more. He haf lif here three year. My family haf lif here three hundred. My grandfather saw the earth swallow the church of San Juan Baptista."

I laughed, until, looking up, I was shocked to see for the first time that his dancing eyes were moist and shining. But almost instantly he jumped up, and declared that I had not seen the garden and the corral, and, linking his arm in mine, swept me like a whirlwind into the patio. For an hour or two he was in his old invincible spirits. I was glad I had said nothing of my visit to Carquinez Springs and of seeing his wife; I determined to avoid it as long as possible; and as he did not again refer to her, except in the past, it was not difficult. At last he infected me with his extravagance, and for a while I forgot even the strangeness of his conduct and his confidences. We walked and talked together as of old. I understood and enjoyed him perfectly, and it was not strange that in the end I began to believe that this strange revelation was a bit of his extravagant acting, got up to amuse me. The coincidence of his story with my own experience was not, after all, such a wonderful thing, considering what must have been the nervous and mental disturbance produced by the earthquake. We dined together, attended only by Pedro, an old half-caste body-servant. It was easy to see that the household was carried on economically, and, from a word or two casually dropped by Enriquez, it appeared that the rancho and a small sum of money were all that he retained from his former fortune when he left the El Bolero. The stock he kept intact, refusing to take the dividend upon it until that collapse of the company should occur which he confidently predicted, when he would make good the swindled stockholders. I had no reason to doubt his perfect faith in this.

The next morning we were up early for a breezy gallop over the three square miles of Enriquez's estate. I was astounded, when I descended to the patio, to find Enriquez already mounted, and carrying before him, astride of the horn of his saddle, a small child,—the identical papoose of my memorable first visit. But the boy was no longer swathed and bandaged, although, for security, his plump little body was engirt by the same sash that encircled his father's own waist. I felt a stirring of self-reproach; I had forgotten all about him! To my suggestion that the exercise might be fatiguing to him, Enriquez shrugged his shoulders:—

"Believe me, no! He is ever with me when I go on the pasear. He is not too yonge. For he shall learn 'to rride, to shoot, and to speak the truth,' even as the Persian chile. Eet ees all I can gif to him."

Nevertheless, I think the boy enjoyed it, and I knew he was safe with such an accomplished horseman as his father. Indeed, it was a fine sight to see them both careering over the broad plain, Enriquez with jingling spurs and whirling riata, and the boy, with a face as composed as his father's, and his tiny hand grasping the end of the flapping rein with a touch scarcely lighter than the skillful rider's own. It was a lovely morning; though warm and still, there was a faint haze—a rare thing in that climate—on the distant range. The sun-baked soil, arid and thirsty from the long summer drought, and cracked into long fissures, broke into puffs of dust, with a slight detonation like a pistol-shot, at each stroke of our pounding hoofs. Suddenly my horse swerved in full gallop, almost lost his footing, "broke," and halted with braced fore feet, trembling in every limb. I heard a shout from Enriquez at the same instant, and saw that he too had halted about a hundred paces from me, with his hand uplifted in warning, and between us a long chasm in the dry earth, extending across the whole field. But the trembling of the horse continued until it communicated itself to me. I was shaking, too, and, looking about for the cause, when I beheld the most weird and remarkable spectacle I had ever witnessed. The whole llano, or plain, stretching to the horizon-line, was DISTINCTLY UNDULATING! The faint haze of the hills was repeated over its surface, as if a dust had arisen from some grinding displacement of the soil. I threw myself from my horse, but the next moment was fain to cling to him, as I felt the thrill under my very feet. Then there was a pause, and I lifted my head to look for Enriquez. He was nowhere to be seen! With a terrible recollection of the fissure that had yawned between us, I sprang to the saddle again, and spurred the frightened beast toward that point. BUT IT WAS GONE, TOO! I rode backward and forward repeatedly along the line where I had seen it only a moment before. The plain lay compact and uninterrupted, without a crack or fissure. The dusty haze that had arisen had passed as mysteriously away; the clear outline of the valley returned; the great field was empty!

Presently I was aware of the sound of galloping hoofs. I

remembered then—what I had at first forgotten—that a few moments before we had crossed an arroyo, or dried bed of a stream, depressed below the level of the field. How foolish that I had not remembered! He had evidently sought that refuge; there were his returning hoofs. I galloped toward it, but only to meet a frightened vaquero, who had taken that avenue of escape to the rancho.

"Did you see Don Enriquez?" I asked impatiently.

I saw that the man's terror was extreme, and his eyes were staring in their sockets. He hastily crossed himself:—

"Ah, God, yes!"

"Where is he?" I demanded.

"Gone!"

"Where?"

He looked at me with staring, vacant eyes, and, pointing to the ground, said in Spanish: "He has returned to the land of his fathers!"

We searched for him that day and the next, when the country was aroused and his neighbors joined in a quest that proved useless. Neither he nor his innocent burden was ever seen again of men. Whether he had been engulfed by mischance in some unsuspected yawning chasm in that brief moment, or had fulfilled his own prophecy by deliberately erasing himself for some purpose known only to himself, no one ever knew. His country-people shook their heads and said "it was like a Saltillo." And the few among his retainers who knew him and loved him, whispered still more ominously: "He will yet return to his land to confound the Americanos."

Yet the widow of Enriquez did NOT marry Professor Dobbs. But she too disappeared from California, and years afterward I was told that she was well known to the ingenuous Parisians as the usual wealthy widow "from South America."

ABOUT THE AUTHOR

 **Francis Bret Harte** (August 25, 1836–May 6, 1902) was an American author and poet, best remembered for his accounts of pioneering life in California.

Born in Albany, New York, Harte moved to California in 1853, later working there in a number of capacities, including miner, teacher, messenger, and journalist. He spent part of his life in the northern California coast town now known as Arcata, at the time it was just a mining camp on Humboldt Bay.

His first literary efforts, including poetry and prose, appeared in The Californian, an early literary journal edited by Charles Henry Webb. In 1868 he became editor of The Overland Monthly, another new literary magazine, but this one more in tune with the pioneering spirit of excitement in California. His story, "The Luck of Roaring Camp," appeared in the magazine's second edition, propelling Harte to nationwide fame.

As an established literary figure, he was appointed to the position of United States Consul in the town of Krefeld, Germany in 1878 and Glasgow in 1880. In 1885 he settled in London. During the thirty years he spent in Europe, he never abandoned writing, and maintained a prodigious output of stories that retained the freshness of his earlier work. He died in England in 1902.

Other books by this author

Openings in the Old Trail
Sally Dows and Other Stories
Maruja
Tales of the Argonauts
Tales of Trail and Town
The Three Partners
Under the Redwoods
By Shore and Sedge
Colonel Starbottle's Client and Other Stories
Clarence
Cressy
Devil's Ford
Frontier Stories
In a Hollow of the Hills
In the Carquinez Woods
Jeff Briggs's Love Story
Snow-Bound at Eagle's
The Argonauts of North Liberty
The Bell-Ringer of Angel's and Other Stories
The Crusade of the Excelsior
The Story of a Mine

Bret Harte

Choose from Thousands of 1stWorldLibrary Classics By

A. M. Barnard
Ada Leverson
Adolphus William Ward
Aesop
Agatha Christie
Alexander Aaronsohn
Alexander Kielland
Alexandre Dumas
Alfred Gatty
Alfred Ollivant
Alice Duer Miller
Alice Turner Curtis
Alice Dunbar
Allen Chapman
Alleyne Ireland
Ambrose Bierce
Amelia E. Barr
Amory H. Bradford
Andrew Lang
Andrew McFarland Davis
Andy Adams
Angela Brazil
Anna Alice Chapin
Anna Sewell
Annie Besant
Annie Hamilton Donnell
Annie Payson Call
Annie Roe Carr
Annonaymous
Anton Chekhov
Archibald Lee Fletcher
Arnold Bennett
Arthur C. Benson
Arthur Conan Doyle
Arthur M. Winfield
Arthur Ransome
Arthur Schnitzler
Arthur Train
Atticus
B.H. Baden-Powell
B. M. Bower
B. C. Chatterjee
Baroness Emmuska Orczy
Baroness Orczy
Basil King
Bayard Taylor
Ben Macomber
Bertha Muzzy Bower
Bjornstjerne Bjornson

Booth Tarkington
Boyd Cable
Bram Stoker
C. Collodi
C. E. Orr
C. M. Ingleby
Carolyn Wells
Catherine Parr Traill
Charles A. Eastman
Charles Amory Beach
Charles Dickens
Charles Dudley Warner
Charles Farrar Browne
Charles Ives
Charles Kingsley
Charles Klein
Charles Hanson Towne
Charles Lathrop Pack
Charles Romyn Dake
Charles Whibley
Charles Willing Beale
Charlotte M. Braeme
Charlotte M. Yonge
Charlotte Perkins Stetson
Clair W. Hayes
Clarence Day Jr.
Clarence E. Mulford
Clemence Housman
Confucius
Coningsby Dawson
Cornelis DeWitt Wilcox
Cyril Burleigh
D. H. Lawrence
Daniel Defoe
David Garnett
Dinah Craik
Don Carlos Janes
Donald Keyhoe
Dorothy Kilner
Dougan Clark
Douglas Fairbanks
E. Nesbit
E. P. Roe
E. Phillips Oppenheim
E. S. Brooks
Earl Barnes
Edgar Rice Burroughs
Edith Van Dyne
Edith Wharton

Edward Everett Hale
Edward J. O'Biren
Edward S. Ellis
Edwin L. Arnold
Eleanor Atkins
Eleanor Hallowell Abbott
Eliot Gregory
Elizabeth Gaskell
Elizabeth McCracken
Elizabeth Von Arnim
Ellem Key
Emerson Hough
Emilie F. Carlen
Emily Bronte
Emily Dickinson
Enid Bagnold
Enilor Macartney Lane
Erasmus W. Jones
Ernie Howard Pie
Ethel May Dell
Ethel Turner
Ethel Watts Mumford
Eugene Sue
Eugenie Foa
Eugene Wood
Eustace Hale Ball
Evelyn Everett-green
Everard Cotes
F. H. Cheley
F. J. Cross
F. Marion Crawford
Fannie E. Newberry
Federick Austin Ogg
Ferdinand Ossendowski
Fergus Hume
Florence A. Kilpatrick
Fremont B. Deering
Francis Bacon
Francis Darwin
Frances Hodgson Burnett
Frances Parkinson Keyes
Frank Gee Patchin
Frank Harris
Frank Jewett Mather
Frank L. Packard
Frank V. Webster
Frederic Stewart Isham
Frederick Trevor Hill
Frederick Winslow Taylor

Friedrich Kerst
Friedrich Nietzsche
Fyodor Dostoyevsky
G.A. Henty
G.K. Chesterton
Gabrielle E. Jackson
Garrett P. Serviss
Gaston Leroux
George A. Warren
George Ade
Geroge Bernard Shaw
George Cary Eggleston
George Durston
George Ebers
George Eliot
George Gissing
George MacDonald
George Meredith
George Orwell
George Sylvester Viereck
George Tucker
George W. Cable
George Wharton James
Gertrude Atherton
Gordon Casserly
Grace E. King
Grace Gallatin
Grace Greenwood
Grant Allen
Guillermo A. Sherwell
Gulielma Zollinger
Gustav Flaubert
H. A. Cody
H. B. Irving
H. C. Bailey
H. G. Wells
H. H. Munro
H. Irving Hancock
H. R. Naylor
H. Rider Haggard
H. W. C. Davis
Haldeman Julius
Hall Caine
Hamilton Wright Mabie
Hans Christian Andersen
Harold Avery
Harold McGrath
Harriet Beecher Stowe
Harry Castlemon
Harry Coghill
Harry Houidini

Hayden Carruth
Helent Hunt Jackson
Helen Nicolay
Hendrik Conscience
Hendy David Thoreau
Henri Barbusse
Henrik Ibsen
Henry Adams
Henry Ford
Henry Frost
Henry James
Henry Jones Ford
Henry Seton Merriman
Henry W Longfellow
Herbert A. Giles
Herbert Carter
Herbert N. Casson
Herman Hesse
Hildegard G. Frey
Homer
Honore De Balzac
Horace B. Day
Horace Walpole
Horatio Alger Jr.
Howard Pyle
Howard R. Garis
Hugh Lofting
Hugh Walpole
Humphry Ward
Ian Maclaren
Inez Haynes Gillmore
Irving Bacheller
Isabel Cecilia Williams
Isabel Hornibrook
Israel Abrahams
Ivan Turgenev
J. G.Austin
J. Henri Fabre
J. M. Barrie
J. M. Walsh
J. Macdonald Oxley
J. R. Miller
J. S. Fletcher
J. S. Knowles
J. Storer Clouston
J. W. Duffield
Jack London
Jacob Abbott
James Allen
James Andrews
James Baldwin

James Branch Cabell
James DeMille
James Joyce
James Lane Allen
James Lane Allen
James Oliver Curwood
James Oppenheim
James Otis
James R. Driscoll
Jane Abbott
Jane Austen
Jane L. Stewart
Janet Aldridge
Jens Peter Jacobsen
Jerome K. Jerome
Jessie Graham Flower
John Buchan
John Burroughs
John Cournos
John F. Kennedy
John Gay
John Glasworthy
John Habberton
John Joy Bell
John Kendrick Bangs
John Milton
John Philip Sousa
John Taintor Foote
Jonas Lauritz Idemil Lie
Jonathan Swift
Joseph A. Altsheler
Joseph Carey
Joseph Conrad
Joseph E. Badger Jr
Joseph Hergesheimer
Joseph Jacobs
Jules Vernes
Julian Hawthrone
Julie A Lippmann
Justin Huntly McCarthy
Kakuzo Okakura
Karle Wilson Baker
Kate Chopin
Kenneth Grahame
Kenneth McGaffey
Kate Langley Bosher
Kate Langley Bosher
Katherine Cecil Thurston
Katherine Stokes
L. A. Abbot
L. T. Meade

L. Frank Baum
Latta Griswold
Laura Dent Crane
Laura Lee Hope
Laurence Housman
Lawrence Beasley
Leo Tolstoy
Leonid Andreyev
Lewis Carroll
Lewis Sperry Chafer
Lilian Bell
Lloyd Osbourne
Louis Hughes
Louis Joseph Vance
Louis Tracy
Louisa May Alcott
Lucy Fitch Perkins
Lucy Maud Montgomery
Luther Benson
Lydia Miller Middleton
Lyndon Orr
M. Corvus
M. H. Adams
Margaret E. Sangster
Margret Howth
Margaret Vandercook
Margaret W. Hungerford
Margret Penrose
Maria Edgeworth
Maria Thompson Daviess
Mariano Azuela
Marion Polk Angellotti
Mark Overton
Mark Twain
Mary Austin
Mary Catherine Crowley
Mary Cole
Mary Hastings Bradley
Mary Roberts Rinehart
Mary Rowlandson
M. Wollstonecraft Shelley
Maud Lindsay
Max Beerbohm
Myra Kelly
Nathaniel Hawthrone
Nicolo Machiavelli
O. F. Walton
Oscar Wilde

Owen Johnson
P.G. Wodehouse
Paul and Mabel Thorne
Paul G. Tomlinson
Paul Severing
Percy Brebner
Percy Keese Fitzhugh
Peter B. Kyne
Plato
Quincy Allen
R. Derby Holmes
R. L. Stevenson
R. S. Ball
Rabindranath Tagore
Rahul Alvares
Ralph Bonehill
Ralph Henry Barbour
Ralph Victor
Ralph Waldo Emmerson
Rene Descartes
Ray Cummings
Rex Beach
Rex E. Beach
Richard Harding Davis
Richard Jefferies
Richard Le Gallienne
Robert Barr
Robert Frost
Robert Gordon Anderson
Robert L. Drake
Robert Lansing
Robert Lynd
Robert Michael Ballantyne
Robert W. Chambers
Rosa Nouchette Carey
Rudyard Kipling
Saint Augustine
Samuel B. Allison
Samuel Hopkins Adams
Sarah Bernhardt
Sarah C. Hallowell
Selma Lagerlof
Sherwood Anderson
Sigmund Freud
Standish O'Grady
Stanley Weyman
Stella Benson
Stella M. Francis

Stephen Crane
Stewart Edward White
Stijn Streuvels
Swami Abhedananda
Swami Parmananda
T. S. Ackland
T. S. Arthur
The Princess Der Ling
Thomas A. Janvier
Thomas A Kempis
Thomas Anderton
Thomas Bailey Aldrich
Thomas Bulfinch
Thomas De Quincey
Thomas Dixon
Thomas H. Huxley
Thomas Hardy
Thomas More
Thornton W. Burgess
U. S. Grant
Upton Sinclair
Valentine Williams
Various Authors
Vaughan Kester
Victor Appleton
Victor G. Durham
Victoria Cross
Virginia Woolf
Wadsworth Camp
Walter Camp
Walter Scott
Washington Irving
Wilbur Lawton
Wilkie Collins
Willa Cather
Willard F. Baker
William Dean Howells
William le Queux
W. Makepeace Thackeray
William W. Walter
William Shakespeare
Winston Churchill
Yei Theodora Ozaki
Yogi Ramacharaka
Young E. Allison
Zane Grey

www.ingramcontent.com/pod-product-compliance
Lightning Source LLC
Chambersburg PA
CBHW050527260626
47157CB00004B/1499